Southern Curses

A MAX PORTER PARANORMAL MYSTERY

Stuart Jaffe

Copyright © 2016 by Stuart Jaffe
Cover art by Jeff Dekal

ISBN 13: 978-1-7337308-8-4

First Edition: May, 2016
First Hardcover Edition: February, 2024

For my beautiful wife, Glory

Also by Stuart Jaffe

Southern Curses

Chapter 1

MAX HAD A BAD FEELING about the party before they ever arrived. Less than five minutes inside, and he knew it would be worse.

"Come on," Sandra had said with her playful cajoling voice. Max had tried to back out of the night, but she wouldn't have it. However, rather than spit out venomous words that would only make him dig in harder, Max's sweet wife knew how to handle him. "It's been ages since we've been to a party."

"The fact that I hate parties might have something to do with that."

She pushed his shoulder. "You do not hate parties."

"I've never liked going out into a big crowd of drunken people."

"What about college? I've heard stories."

"Most of which have been exaggerated. Besides, that was college. I did a lot of stupid stuff back then. I'm more refined now."

Sandra laughed. "More refined than what? A grizzly bear with gas?"

Max pinched his waist line. "I may not be in perfect shape, but I'm no bear."

"You're my bear — a teddy bear."

He wrapped his arms around her. "All right. I know where this is all going. I've already lost this argument before it started, didn't I?"

"Yup." She pecked his cheek. "Try to have some fun tonight. Maria is a good person and it was kind of her to invite us."

They drove up into Mount Tabor, a wealthy suburban area far enough from downtown Winston-Salem to protect it from being urbanized, close enough to go in for a ballgame or a street fair, if the mood struck. Max tried to hide his distaste but wriggled in his suit and tie.

Maria Cortez-Kane lived in a modest house — modest by Mount Tabor standards. Sitting on the top of a manicured hill, the brick house boasted a four-column entryway like a bank. Four bedrooms, three full bathrooms, and a lavish kitchen — all meticulously appointed to impress. In the backyard, an in-ground swimming pool glistened under the moonlight.

Max leaned in a doorway with a glass of wine in his hand. He gazed around the high-ceilinged living room, hoping to catch a glimpse of his wife but seeing more sparkling diamonds and flashy gold watches than anything else. *Strange,* he thought. *We have money and a beautiful house and everything these people have — not to the same degree, but we have it — yet somehow I still don't feel part of this world.* Not that Max wanted to be a part of such a world, but rather, he found it odd that money alone wasn't enough to gain access to the rich.

With the way business was going, though, he might not have to worry about such things for long. Over the last six months, a total of three clients had walked through their doors, none of whom produced much in the way of income or interest. Having a bunch of money was nice, but Max spent a lot of time calculating how many years before it all dried up. No way would it last the rest of their lives. Maybe not even ten years unless they started getting some real income.

He wished Marshall Drummond would stop by. His partner, a ghost from the 1940s and a top-notch detective, would make the party interesting or, at least, distract him from his worries. But Sandra made Max promise to leave the ghost at home. Not that Max could have forced Drummond to come. That ghost did whatever he wanted to do and the heck with everybody else.

"It's Max, right?" a joyful voice said. "Pleasure to meet you. I'm Brian Dorsett."

Brian thrust out a meaty hand and gripped Max in a vice handshake. The man looked to be in his forties, a bit overweight, and rosy with drink. His suit fit right in with the house — meticulous and expensive.

"Nice to meet you." Though Max wanted to go home, he knew how to be polite. "How is it you know me?"

Brian sipped vodka from a short glass. "I don't, really. Just your name and what you look like. Part of the deal, y'know. I've got to keep up with who all is doing what all and where all."

"The deal?"

"Sorry. I sometimes get ahead of a conversation. I'm already in Mexico and you haven't even hit the border yet." He laughed and placed a hand on Max's shoulder. "No need to look so confused. I work for one of the big families."

"Oh?" Three families ruled over Winston-Salem. The Reynolds family had made its name in tobacco. The Hanes family built its empire through underwear, socks, and such. Max knew little about these two. The third family, the Hull family, Max knew too much about. The Hull fortune came about through dark magic, evil curses, and worse. "Is this some kind of threat? Tucker Hull send you?"

Brian's mouth soured as he glared at Max. "We're watching you." Then he burst into laughter. "No, no, I work for the Reynolds family. Handle insurance issues and such for the estate. That's why I got to stay on top of what goes on and who goes on in this town. You really thought I worked for Hull? I'd never go near a Hull. Those folks are freaky." He slapped Max on the back and handed over his business card. "Boy, I had you shaking."

In a near-monotone, Max said, "Yeah, you got me good."

"Never heard of Tucker Hull, though. I thought the young one ran the family now, um, Terrance Hull."

"Oh, is that his name? Terrance?" Max hoped Brian was too drunk to remember any of this in the morning. Terrance had given up power to the family when the original patriarch, Tucker, was summoned back from the grave. Max shook off his thoughts — he had no need for the Hull family to be in his head during a party.

"Will you look at that?" Brian said, lifting his pinky from his vodka glass to point across the room at their host.

Maria Cortez-Kane stood amongst several women, Sandra included, with a bright smile and gracious charm. Based on the little he knew from Sandra, Max found Maria to be a fascinating balance of opposites. On one hand, she was the demure wife of Norman Kane, a successful contracts attorney. On the other hand, she was a New Age nut who flowed like a river with no banks — wherever life took her.

Brian appeared more interested in Maria's ample cleavage. "I'm telling you, that woman has it all. If I were her baby, I'd breast feed until I was a teen. I mean, that mama could rock me to sleep any night."

Max tried to hold his face still. He had no such luck with his mouth. "That's the most disturbing thing I've heard all year."

"Oh, don't be such a prude. Look at that body. Besides, I heard she's into all sorts of weird, kinky stuff. She'd be right at home with your Hull friends."

Not wanting to embarrass Sandra, Max looked for a polite getaway. He found his solution in Brian's near-empty glass. "How about a toast?"

"Excellent idea." Brian raised his glass. "To women. May they always accept a man like me into their beds." He tipped the last of his vodka back and missed the fact that Max did not share the toast.

"Looks like you've gone dry."

Brian puckered his lips as he contemplated the empty glass. "That I have." With another slap on Max's back, he chuckled. "I suppose I'll have to remedy this situation. Can I get you anything?"

"No, thanks. I'm all set."

As Brian weaved toward the bar, Max broke off in the opposite direction. He worked his way down a crowded hall and around a corner, hoping to find a quiet area to sit out the rest of the evening. Instead, he entered a room with an enormous flatscreen television and a dozen rowdy men watching a football game — a rerun from the 1970s. The man holding court in the center of an extra-long couch was Norman Kane. When he grew silent to watch the next play, the men around him followed suit. As the play unfolded, the men raised their voices until reaching a crescendo of excitement.

No way would Max stay there. He spied a staircase off to the right and made his escape before anybody decided to be friendly enough to invite him over. He strolled down a perfect hallway with waxed, hardwood floors and just enough photos to be warm but not cluttered.

A door on his left stood ajar. He peeked in and saw a desk and floor-to-ceiling bookshelves. Flicking on the ceiling lamp — a colorful, domed piece that brought the room a rich sense of depth — Max perused the shelves.

Several held nothing but thick, legal reference books. These played opposite well-endowed fertility statues and a golden Buddha. Max smirked. That was the Cortez-Kane family in a nutshell.

Sitting on one shelf, directly in front of him, Max saw a framed black-and-white photograph. It was a portrait of a young woman in formal dress. She looked sternly at the camera with eyes so dark they might have been inked in.

Max picked up the frame and tilted it, trying to see if the impression of pen could be found on the smooth surface of the photo. Nothing. That suggested the woman's eyes really were that dark. Strange.

Cocking his head to the side to read the titles on the lower shelves, Max's heart chilled. *The Lore of Witchcraft. Winston-Salem Witch. The Basic Grimoire. Covens.* Then on the next shelf over — *Spells for Summer. Binding Spell Primer. Light Magik.*

Max straightened and scanned the rest of the room. Candles, chalk, salt, and other witchcraft paraphernalia had been neatly organized on the desk. A double-ringed circle had been painted on the floor. With that circle, a person could write a spell with chalk, cast it, and later, clear the floor for a new spell.

Max hurried downstairs and sought Sandra. He found her in

the kitchen gawking over an eight-burner stove. "We have to go now," he said.

She looked up at him, her scowl disappearing as she took in his appearance. "What happened?"

"I'll tell you in the car."

Sandra pushed through the crowd to give Maria a hug and an apology. From the sympathetic pout Maria made, Max guessed his wife claimed he wasn't feeling well — or that he was being an ass and these were the crosses a wife must bear. Either way, when she finished, she grabbed her coat and stormed by Max on her way out.

Once they were on the road, Max told her everything he had seen.

"That's it?" Sandra said. "That's why we had to leave?"

"Did you hear me? Maria's a witch."

"I knew that already."

"Huh? You did?"

"Yes, honey. I've been to that house before. I've seen her books and stuff. Oh, and I'm not an idiot."

"I never said that. Don't start picking a fight where there isn't one."

"Then don't treat me like a child."

Max opened his mouth; then wisely shut it. He thought he had been saving his wife from danger. How had it all become a blunder that was his fault? "Should we go back?"

"After I lied to her that you were ill?"

"I'm sorry," he said, wondering how things turned around that he was apologizing.

Though Sandra's jaw tensed, her eyes softened. "I know you didn't mean it like that, but you should know better. Don't you trust me? Trust my judgment?"

"Of course, I do. But you never said anything before about her being a witch, so I figured you didn't know. When I saw all of that spell casting stuff, I thought we were in danger."

"From Maria? She'd never hurt me. She'd never hurt anybody. Look, honey, she's my friend. We've been living here for years now, and I hardly know anybody. She's the first person that's not you who I can call a friend."

"What about Drummond?"

"Fine. She's the first *living* person. And tonight meant a lot to me. She invited us to that party. All we had to do was have a good time."

"And I ruined it."

Sandra lowered her head into her hands and rubbed her temples. "It wasn't you. I mean, not directly. It's all this Hull business. Ever since we moved to North Carolina, we've had to live under their shadow. That's why Maria is so special. She's not part of any of that."

"She's a witch. That kind of means Hull, at the least, knows about her."

"I doubt it. She's not a powerful player or anything like that. Most of the spells she's ever tried to cast have fizzled out. She even told me her mentor is considering dropping her as a student."

Max glanced in his rearview mirror. A car had pulled out behind them and sped up. "Crap," he said. "I think I'm about to get a ticket." The car continued to accelerate. Its high-beams popped on, blinding Max. "This is ridiculous. Is he going to pull me over or not?"

Sandra leaned back to look out the rear window. "I don't think that's a cop."

The car gunned its engine and rammed them. Max gripped the steering wheel as the car behind them hit again. With his brain rattling around his skull, he tried to focus on the road. He pressed hard on the gas, but their attacker matched him, then sped up and smashed them a third time.

They were on local roads with forests and fields, homes and churches lining the way. He pressed on, hoping he'd reach the on-ramp for US-40 — a major highway that would allow him to floor the gas without hurting anybody. He never got the chance.

The car behind pulled into the oncoming lane and zoomed up beside him. Max looked over and saw the driver looking back. A pale-skinned man with a deep scar running from the corner of his eye down to his jaw. He grinned at Max, revealing a silver incisor, before he wrenched the wheel over.

The man's car slammed into Max's. Max had been so distracted by the man's appearance that he lost control of the car. Sandra screamed as they busted through a guard rail and over the side. They bounced down, straight for a tree. Max had time enough to spin the car to the right, protecting Sandra's side from the main impact.

He heard the crumpling door. He heard the shattering glass. He saw nothing.

It all went dark.

Chapter 2

BEFORE HE OPENED HIS EYES, Max heard the quiet murmurs, the low television sounds, and the steady beeps that clued him in to his location — a hospital. He could smell it, too — that off-putting, antiseptic odor, a concoction of disinfectants and illness. Peeking through one eye confirmed his suspicion. *Yeah, I'm in a hospital.*

He sat up, surprised that his head did not ring nor did his muscles complain, and swung his legs off the bed. No broken bones. If he had managed to escape serious injury, then Sandra must be okay, too. With a sigh, he got to his feet and crossed the room to look out the window.

Hanes Mall spread out before him along with numerous restaurants and box stores as well as plenty of traffic. "Guess I'm at Forsyth Medical." The other major hospital in the area was Wake Forest Baptist, but his view would have been of homes and trees as well as plenty of traffic.

"You're finally up," Marshall Drummond said as he floated next to Max. He wore the same clothes he had died in — an everyday suit with a long coat and a Fedora. That constant attire now covered Max with a bit of comfort. Drummond gave Max an awkward wink. "Enjoying the view?"

"Sure. I love to look out at a shopping Mecca. Or did you mean your fine self?"

Drummond chuckled — which was odd because he didn't return with a jibe. "How are you feeling?"

"Okay, I guess."

"Really? Completely normal?"

"Anxious to get out of here. Sandra's okay, right?"

"She's perfectly fine."

"Then will you go tell her I'm awake and ... what's with that look?"

Drummond tilted his Fedora over his eyes. "I ain't got any kind of look. You sure you don't feel any different or anything?"

Max went to slap the window but halted when he heard a gasp from behind. Sandra stood in the doorway. She had dropped a cup of coffee and it had formed a brown puddle in front of her. Her eyes glistened, but there was no joy in her face. Instead, her chin quivered as she gazed at the hospital bed.

Max followed her eyes. He was still in the bed. That is, his body was in the bed.

Reality spun out with a chill across his heart. He looked to Drummond, but the ghost averted his eyes. "Am I? I mean, did I ..."

Sandra covered her mouth as she rushed to the bedside. "Max? Can you hear me?"

"You know I can. I'm right here."

She glowered at him before turning back to the body. "Max. Wake up."

"What is this?" Max asked Drummond. "Am I dead?"

Drummond reached out and clasped Max by the shoulder. His ghostly hands didn't go through Max nor did Max feel the usual cold whenever accidentally passing through a ghost. Drummond's hands simply rested on Max's shoulders — solid and without cold or pain. "I'm sorry, pal."

"No," Max said, wriggling away from Drummond. "Sandra, come on. This isn't right. I'm not dead. I can't be dead. It was a stupid car wreck. We didn't flip or anything. We didn't explode. We just hit a tree. I can't be dead from that."

Sandra kissed the forehead of the Max in the hospital bed. Then she looked at Max's ghost. "Honey," she said. "I love you. But you need to accept what has happened. It's important, so that you can move on. Otherwise, you'll be stuck here."

"This doesn't make sense. We hit a tree. Not even a big one.

We weren't going that fast."

"Please, Max. You've got to pay attention. If you don't move on, you'll be here all the time. You understand? You'll be stuck. And, honey, you'll be haunting me. Is that what you want? To haunt your wife?"

"I'm not dead. I don't feel dead."

Drummond said, "How's that supposed to feel? Listen to your wife. She's right. I can touch you without hurting you or myself. You know what that means."

Pointing to Drummond's pocket, Max said, "Is Leed in there?" When alive, Leed had been a witch hunter and an expert in the occult. His horrible death resulted in his soul becoming a glowing blob, and Drummond let Leed reside in his pocket — at least, that was all Max had ever seen of the man.

"Leed's always with me."

"Well, if I'm dead how come I can't hear him or see him?"

"You can't hear him because he ain't talkin' right now. He's not like a full ghost. It takes a lot for him to partake in the mortal world. More and more lately. He hasn't talked in a few days, even to me. But you want to see him? Sure."

Drummond scooped his hand into his pocket, pulled it out, and opened his palm up.

Max grinned. "I don't see anything. He's not there."

"That's odd. You should be able to see him."

Max stomped around the room. "Get a doctor in here. Get somebody to examine me." He stopped short and looked across the bed while avoiding looking at himself. "There. That machine is beeping. Isn't that my heart?"

Sandra looked at the heart monitor. Wiping her eyes, she nodded. "That's strange. I mean, you've been in a coma for three days. When I saw you as a ghost, I assumed you had died while I was getting coffee. I didn't even notice." A smile crept onto her lips. "Honey, it's beeping. Your heart is still beeping."

She dropped to the bed and hugged him. Max stepped beside her. "I know that's my body and all, but I'm really over here."

"I can't hug you that way." Her smile drifted into a frown. "Why are you that way? You shouldn't be a ghost unless you died."

"I don't know. Drummond?"

The detective shrugged. "Never seen anything like this."

Max lifted his hand, noticing for the first time that he could see through it. It felt real. He waved it around and he could feel the air shift along his skin. Yet it had to be some kind of illusion like a phantom leg. *Except I'm the phantom.*

Drummond floated toward the ceiling as he thought. Max wondered if he, too, could float but decided against trying just yet. Sandra would not appreciate the image. Drummond snapped his fingers. "Maybe something happened to you during the accident."

That brought Max's thoughts back into focus. "That wasn't an accident."

Sandra said, "I know that guy rammed us, but it seemed more like road rage than anything deliberate."

"I saw him when he pulled up next to us. I saw his face. I'm telling you, we were targeted."

"Honey, don't start looking for trouble."

"I'm not, but it's coming for us."

"Everything's been quiet. We're not even on a case."

"Just because things have been quiet lately doesn't mean our enemies have given up. Tucker Hull is out there, and you know he wants to hurt us."

Drummond said, "I'm afraid he's right, doll. You both know how serious the Hull family can be. I suspect this was meant to be a warning shot over the bow, but it went a bit further than they had planned. Now that you're awake, you should expect to be hearing from Hull soon. Probably through our old pal, Mr. Modesto."

Sandra wrinkled her nose. "I'd be fine with never seeing that man again. Ever."

"It's strange, though," Max said. "Why a warning shot at all? We've been at odds with them for a few years, now. There's no need to warn us. We know Tucker wants us gone."

Drummond said, "Then what? You think he really tried to kill you in such a clumsy way? I don't believe that. When he actually wants to kill you both, he'll do it with magic."

"I don't know. But since we don't have a case, at least this is the only thing we'll have to focus on."

The room door opened. "Perhaps I can help," an elderly woman said as she entered. Max felt a lump sink into his gut. He knew this woman, this witch, and all the problems she brought with her — Mother Hope.

Drummond shook his head at Max. "You had to say something."

Chapter 3

MOTHER HOPE WALKED TO ONE of two chairs set under the flatscreen television. She wore enough scarves and jangling jewelry to fill a costume shop or play the part of *cliché gypsy #2* in a bad horror movie. She moved her small, hunched body in short steps, each motion implying frailty and weakness. All of it was a lie. Max knew this woman had great power within her — not just her abilities with spells, but also as the leader of the Magi Group, a secret organization devoted to combating families like the Hulls from abusing magic.

Behind her, a large black man stood with a slight bend. Leon Moore. Though he worked as a librarian at Wake Forest University, his position in the Magi Group had caused Max plenty of trouble — usually under the guise of attempting to help.

Mother Hope made a vague hand gesture. "Wait out in the hall. Us ladies need to chat."

Leon bowed his head a fraction before walking out. As Mother Hope settled in a chair, Max pointed at her and said, "I've got no use for you. Get the hell out of here."

Mother Hope did not react. Drummond said, "You're a ghost now. She can't hear or see you."

"My wife can. Hon, translate for me."

Sandra crossed her arms and leveled a stern look at Mother Hope. "In case you're planning on something violent, you should know that we're not alone in here."

The old woman glanced around the room. "Oh, I know that. Is Marshall Drummond here as well?"

"He is."

"Good. Then you all can hear what I have to say."

Sandra raised a hand to stop Max and Drummond from talking. "Make it fast. I doubt they have much patience at the moment. I know I don't."

"Mrs. Porter, you and I have not had many chances to talk. Most of my dealings have been with your husband. So, I will assume you are unaware of how to behave around me, and that is the reason for your unacceptable attitude." Before Sandra could snap off a quick-witted rebuttal, Mother Hope said, "I arranged for your car accident as well as your husband's current predicament. If you continue to be rude and unmannerly towards me, you'll find that I can end Max's life as easily as I have suspended it."

Though her jaw remained clenched, Sandra forced a smile and sat in the other chair. "In that case, I imagine there's a reason behind all this, and that you are here for more than gloating."

"Much more."

Max paced the room. "Don't trust a thing she says."

Drummond settled back against the wall and snickered. "Do you honestly think your wife needs advice from you on how to handle Mother Hope? I mean look at the evidence — you're the one who's dead."

As she spoke, Mother Hope shuffled over to Max's body. "I do hope you weren't hurt in the accident."

"No," Sandra said. "My husband saw to that. He loves me very much."

"Damn right I do," Max said, still pacing.

Mother Hope raised an eyebrow. "We arranged for your accident so that Max would be put in a hospital. I needed access to his body, and I didn't think that would happen without him being unconscious."

"What did you do to him?" Sandra asked.

"Of course, we could have grabbed him off the street or broke into your home and took him, but those actions would have most likely brought the police into the situation. Having them poking about a criminal investigation was unacceptable.

The Hull family has too many connections there. More than us. This way, it was an unfortunate accident. The police filled out a few reports, and that was that."

"Answer me — what did you do to my husband?"

"I cursed him, of course." Mother Hope pulled back Max's hospital gown. When she passed her hand over the right side of his chest, a faint circle with small markings glowed red like a brand.

As the mark grew brighter, Max felt a sting in his chest that quickly become a harsh burn.

"Stop it," Sandra said, her eyes on Max as he clutched his ghostly chest.

Mother Hope covered the body back up and returned to her chair. "This is your fault — all of you. Your little trio has been meddling in the Hull situation for too long. It's hastened events that we thought we had taken care of and forced us to act faster than we intended." Squinting at Sandra, she went on, "The situation is coming to a head, and if the world is ever to be rid of the Hull family, now is the time to strike."

"I'll show you a strike," Max said and charged forward. He pulled back a fist and punched at Mother Hope's chest. Two feet ahead of her, his fist slammed into a hard wall of pain. Electricity jangled up his arm and forced his mouth shut, his teeth gnashing into each other. He flailed backward into Drummond's arms.

"Easy there," Drummond said, setting Max back on his feet. "You'll never be able to hit her like that."

Mother Hope tapped one of the amulets around her neck. "Well, well. It feels as if your husband now knows what it's like to come in contact with a protection ward."

"You okay, hon?" Sandra asked.

Max rubbed his sore hand. "No. None of this is okay."

Sandra turned back to Mother Hope. "You are wasting our time and annoying us. You've cursed my husband. Why? What does it do?"

"If we are to defeat the Hulls, not just set them back but defeat them, then we have no choice but to go for the head.

We were planning on taking out Terrance Hull once he truly took over the business, but you three started helping them acquire the necessary items to resurrect Tucker Hull."

Mother Hope paused. After a few seconds, Sandra said, "If you're waiting for me to apologize, I won't. We were trying to survive our own troubles. Finding those objects for the Hulls meant we continued to live."

"Maybe so. Maybe you would have lived a better life had you not cooperated with that family. Still, here we are. Thanks to you, Tucker has returned. But Tucker cannot be defeated in any conventional manner. He is a being both dead and alive. He exists in both realms, and thus must be defeated in both realms in order to truly be destroyed."

"You cursed Max, so he would fight Tucker in the afterlife?"

Mother Hope snarled. "I cursed Max because he deserved it." Sandra jumped at the woman's fierceness. Then, in a calmer voice, Mother Hope said, "I do not need nor do I want your husband to fight Tucker Hull. Even if he was willing, he would be no match. But he does need to serve a purpose.

"After many months of searching, I have uncovered a rare spell that I believe will solve our Tucker Hull problem. The spell requires casting by powerful witches in both realms — the living and the dead. Both witches must also be connected in some way with the target. The stronger the connection the better.

"Now, the living realm is an easy matter. I have a strong connection of hatred towards all the Hulls, and I am a powerful witch. But I need a witch on the other side as well. One who is capable of casting the spell and has an equal hatred for Tucker that she would be willing to do it. There's only one who fits that description."

Max halted his pacing. His arms dropped. "You have got to be kidding."

"Your husband will use his great skill in uncovering people and information, and he will find the Hull family's former witch-on-retainer, Dr. Ashley Connor."

"No. Absolutely not." Max looked to Drummond. "This is

nuts."

Drummond pursed his lips, then shook his head. "What can you do? You're cursed, right?"

Sandra nodded. "This curse — you'll remove it after he finds Dr. Connor?"

"Of course, dear," Mother Hope said. "The curse keeps him in this state of living and dead. The rest of his body, other than a few bruises, appears to be healthy and fine. Once the curse is removed, he'll wake from his coma and you both can go about your lives knowing that the Hulls will never be a problem for you again."

"But why Dr. Connor? Surely, the Magi Group has plenty of powerful witches that are dead and available."

"Not so. We move on when we die."

Drummond said, "And Dr. Connor was murdered by the Hulls. An angry, murdered witch won't be moving on anytime soon. She'll be around here somewhere."

"To be perfectly clear, though," Mother Hope continued, "your husband has defied me and caused me many problems. If not for the fact that his goals aligned with mine, I would have seen him hurt long ago. As it stands, consider this a punishment. And what better punishment than to force him to work with a witch he abhors?"

Max clenched his fists. "Hon, please slap that old woman for me."

Sandra suppressed a smile. "I don't think Max is feeling too cooperative at the moment."

Again, the fierce side of Mother Hope erupted. "Well, he better change his mind. Because when I remove the curse, I can just as easily send him to the realm of death as I can the living. And nobody will believe he was murdered by magic. In fact, considering the usual outcome for coma patients, nobody will bother to look into it at all. Just another unfortunate tragedy due to drunk driving. You were returning from a party the night of your accident, right?"

Max saw Sandra's fingers tense, and he thought she really would slap the old witch. Instead, she put out her hand. "I think we understand the situation quite well. You can trust we'll do everything possible to find Dr. Connor for you."

Mother Hope took Sandra's hand and gave it a light motion. "I have no doubts."

"We'd like some privacy now. We'll report the moment we learn of anything."

"No need." Mother Hope stood and brushed her backside while her numerous bracelets clanged against each other. She then walked to the door and gave it a single knock. "I have my own people for that purpose."

Before the door had fully opened, Max heard the *click-clack* of sharp, high heels. A petite, blond doctor entered. Her hair had been pulled back into a bun so tight it stretched her skin. Max would never forget the sound of that woman's heels when she had demolished his office computers while Mother Hope watched and warned. Though small like Mother Hope, the high-heeled woman was equally dangerous.

Mother Hope pushed the door closed. "I believe you know Dr. Fremont."

"Yes," Sandra growled.

"I've seen to it that she has been assigned to this floor of the hospital. Max will be one of her patients. She's a well-respected and capable doctor, and as long as you do what you are supposed to do, she will take good care of Max."

"But should we do anything you don't like, you'll kill him."

Mother Hope winced at Sandra's words. "Murder is not an easy thing, and death is not a judgment I will easily pass upon another. Even Tucker Hull's second death, which I pray will be soon, is not something we take lightly. It would be with a heavy heart that I would have to fulfill any threat to Max. But then, all leaders must learn to live with a heavy heart. So, yes, comply with my plans, and you'll not only save your husband's life, but you will also destroy your enemy." To Dr. Fremont, Mother Hope said, "Take care of these people, and report everything they say and do to me."

Gazing once across the room, Mother Hope made an odd noise in her throat like a creaking ship before leaving. Dr.

Fremont followed her out.

The moment the door closed, Sandra rushed over to Max's body and checked his chest. No sign of the cursed mark could be seen. "Are you okay? Do you feel strange or anything?"

Despite his anger, Max laughed. "You mean other than being a ghost?"

Sandra's shoulders drooped. "Yeah, other than that." She pressed the palm of her hand against her eyes. "What are we going to do? This is nuts."

"No more than usual."

Drummond adjusted his hat and slid closer. "I've got to side with Max on this one, doll. We can handle this just fine. We've been through this kind of thing before."

"No," Sandra said. "We've never been through something like this. Witches, ghosts, curses — sure. That's nothing new. But Max being cursed into this half-alive, half-dead state. That is not business as usual."

"I know, hon." Max reached out to comfort her, but she pulled away.

"I don't think the deep-bone chill of a ghost touch is what I need right now."

Drummond brought his hands together in one loud clap. "Before you two work yourselves into a fight or something worse like a bunch of mushy love talk, we've got a witch to go find."

"Yeah," said Max. "And considering that she hates us, it won't be easy."

Chapter 4

MAX, SANDRA, AND DRUMMOND spent an hour discussing the situation. Most of their talk resulted in grumbling and sharp barbs of wit tossed in the direction of Mother Hope. But eventually, they settled onto a clear path — Drummond was to find Dr. Connor by searching the Other, the ghost-only plane of existence that resided between the corporeal realm and that of those who had moved on; Sandra was to dig up all she could find on Max's curse and the possible ways to free him that did not result in his death. Max also asked if Sandra had notified his mother of what had happened.

"No," she said. "I know I should, but when I do tell her, she's going to hop on the first flight over. I don't want to have to deal with her. Not right now. I figured if you die, I could deal with her then, and if you live, there'd be nothing to tell."

"She's my mother."

"What do you want me to say? 'Oh, hi Mrs. Porter. Thought I'd call because your son's been cursed by a psychotic do-gooder witch.' You think that's a good idea?"

"Maybe not those exact words."

By the time they agreed to call Max's mother only if he died and then broke off for their separate assignments, noon had come and gone. They still had hours to make some progress, though. Max had no doubt that both Sandra and Drummond shared the urgency he felt. However, no matter how greatly they could empathize, they weren't the one with the curse. Drummond had been cursed before, he knew exactly what Max was going through, yet even so, Max still wondered if a ghost could truly understand. Except he was a ghost now, too. If he could spend his time moping about feeling alone, then another ghost should also be able to have emotions.

He tried to shove away these thoughts. He was simply frustrated, and it made his mind wander into ridiculous hypotheticals and manufactured concerns. He needed to do something. Unfortunately, his options were limited.

Because he wasn't really dead, he could not access the Other with Drummond. Though even if he could manage that feat, he discovered quite fast and painfully that his ghostly form was tethered to his cursed body. It appeared he could go anywhere within the boundaries of the hospital. However, if he tried to leave the building, he felt a vice grip seize his head and start to pull. The further he went beyond the hospital, the worse the pain. Thus, he stayed behind while Sandra and Drummond did all the leg work.

Standing alone in his hospital room, Max stared at his body. He could have roamed the halls, but after attempting it once, he decided that had been enough. The halls of the hospital were stuffed with dead people. Seeing them wormed under his skin. Worse, he thought if he spent too much time with them, he might lose that sensation. He might get comfortable with the dead. While he had no proof, he thought that the closer he came to the realm of the dead, the harder it might be to bring him back to the living.

"Look at you," he said to his body. "Another fine mess you've gotten us into." He did not laugh. Didn't even crack a morbid smile.

He had already adjusted to the sensations of being a ghost. Passing through objects caused him no feeling at all. If he wanted to actually touch something, it merely required a small amount of concentration. However, the pain of coming into contact with the solid world shocked him.

He knew from working with Drummond that touching things caused pain, had seen it on the old ghost's face, but he had no idea what the experience was like until he attempted to press his hand against the wall. His fingers burned as if he had placed them against a hot stove. Shooting bolts of pain strafed up his spine right into the back of his head. If he had a stomach, he would have thrown up.

All the times Drummond had touched the corporeal world in order to protect or help or outright save Sandra and Max, he had endured this kind of pain. Max wished he could buy the man a drink — a double-shot of whiskey. Drummond would appreciate the gesture even if he couldn't partake in the drinking.

The other aspect of being a ghost that came as a surprise was the loneliness. Max had only been in this state for a few hours, and he already wanted to tear down the walls. Drummond had endured decades before Max freed him from his curse. No wonder most ghosts are haunting people. They're bored out of their minds.

Stuck in the hospital was bad enough for regular patients. Stuck in the hospital as a ghost, especially when there were important things to be done outside of the building, that was sheer torture. Probably part of the reason Mother Hope set things up that way.

An hour later, when his door opened, Max had to hold back from rushing across the room and hugging his visitor. When Peanut Butter entered the room, Max's heart swelled and he zoomed into the corner so as not to accidentally bump the boy. He didn't want PB running off scared.

Not that the boy would. Before Max had hired him to do odd jobs and general help, PB lived on the streets of Winston-Salem. The kid was tough. Still, he was a boy. Perhaps that's why Max always thought of him and his partner, Jammer J, as the Sandwich Boys. Not simply because of the obvious PB and J of their names, but because they were so young.

PB glanced in the hall a moment before pulling a chair beside Max's slumbering body. His thin fingers fidgeted with his shirt before reaching out and patting Max's arm. Two quick pats and PB slipped his hand away.

He cleared his throat. "Hey, Ghostman." PB knew that Max could see Drummond — at least, he knew Max believed that.

"Hey, kid," Max said, though the boy could not hear him.

"Crappy what happened to you. Sorry about it all. Don't you worry though. I'm gonna make sure Ms. Sandra is taken care of. Me and J, we'll do whatever we can to help her out. You got my word."

"That's kind of you."

"I mean, you been real good to me. I don't forget that stuff. Not just the little things you did, neither. The coffee and bagels when I was alone and all, well, that was cool, but you took a chance on me. Give me this job with real pay and everything. Jammer J and I, you know, we don't waste that money. We been saving it. Got a bank account and everything. We even went in together and got an apartment."

PB looked around before leaning in closer. In a soft voice, he said, "Don't tell nobody. I won't be any use to you, telling you what's going on the street and all, if they think I'm suddenly a rich man. I mean, don't get the wrong idea or nothing. This place ain't nice at all. It's a real hole. But we can afford it, and I don't care if it's got cockroaches and mice. It's a roof over my head when it rains. And when it's cold outside, I got some warmth, too. Anyway, I owe that to you and I wanted to thank you."

"No need to thank me," Max said, his mouth open in a wide grin. "You earn your pay all the time."

"I don't want you thinking I'm getting all sappy and stuff, but for an old guy, you're pretty cool. I think if one of my parents had been like you, I wouldn't have ended up like I did."

PB lowered his head and closed his eyes. He said nothing for several minutes. In the quiet, Max watched and held still. He wanted to speak — really, he wanted PB to hear him — to let PB know that his words did not fall away into nothingness. But as he stood there watching, he suspected that PB preferred his words to be lost.

"You know what?" PB said, his voice breaking through like a sudden disturbance in an empty church. "I've done some bad things. I mean I'm sure you think you know what a guy like me has got to do to survive the streets, but that ain't what I'm talking about. I'm talking before the streets, back when I had a home and a mom and a dad and all that crap. I did a real bad thing back then. Maybe if you had been around back then, none of it would've happened. But I want you to know about it. I really do. I want you to know because you put your trust in me. That whole thing with that haunted house — if Jammer J and I hadn't done our part, you could've been killed. That's serious trust."

He peeked at the door and took a shivering breath. "So, you ought to know the kind of person I am — good and bad and all. Especially since I think some of that past is on its way after me."

"Whatever it is, kid, you're part of the business now. That's our family. We'll help you out."

A knock at the door jolted PB to his feet. The door swung open and a stern woman walked in. She had blond hair closely buzzed in the back with sharp, pointed ends on the cropped sides. Her grim, dark eyes stood out from her pale skin. Max knew the woman right away, but PB had no clue, and Max had no way to warn him. Cecily Hull had come to visit.

"Who are you?" she demanded.

PB straightened and his chin lifted. "I'm a friend of Max. Who the hell are you?"

"Where's Sandra? I know her too well to think she'd abandon her husband."

PB shrugged. "Haven't seen her."

"Can you go find her for me?"

"No."

Cecily pulled back. "What does that mean? You can't or you won't?"

"Look, lady, you act like a rich, stuck-up ass, so I ain't helping you with nothing."

Max suppressed a laugh until he remembered that nobody could hear him. Then he let it roar out.

Cecily dug into her purse and pulled out a hundred dollar bill. "If I give you this, will you deliver a message for me?"

"I don't want your money. This room's for friends and family. You obviously ain't either."

She never faltered. She simply slid the money back into her purse. "You are fortunate that today I have serious matters to deal with. Otherwise, I think I'd enjoy seeing you suffer the consequences of your rudeness." Her cold delivery had the desired effect upon PB. "You tell Sandra Porter that Cecily Hull wants to speak with her on an important matter. She knows how to contact me." Cecily turned toward the door, paused, and added, "And she better."

As Cecily walked out, Max started to follow. At the door, however, he stopped. He looked at PB. The boy had something important to unload, something he had been building up to. But Cecily had interrupted and the momentum had disappeared. Would he try again?

Following Cecily was important, too — it could not have been a coincidence that she arrived on the same day that Mother Hope had visited. Drummond taught Max a long time ago the likelihood of such things truly being coincidences. "Never happens," the detective had said.

Cecily, then. If PB truly wanted to share something with Max, he would do so when Max was conscious. For that matter, Max had to admit that he felt a bit slimy eavesdropping on PB's private words. The boy had no reason to think Max was listening.

Stepping into the hall, Max braced himself for the claustrophobic crowd of ghosts. Men and women of all ages filled the hall like transparent statues. They loitered in the halls, paying particular attention to the living, and watched life trickle by.

Weaving through the throngs, Max followed Cecily to the elevators. He kept bumping into the other ghosts but managed to avoid passing through more than a few humans. When Cecily boarded the elevator, Max joined her. But when the doors closed and the elevator descended, Max passed through the ceiling and remained floating in the elevator shaft.

His head spun as his instincts told him he would plummet to his death. He paddled his arms and legs about as if drowning. When nothing happened — neither moving toward the walls nor tumbling toward the bottom — he started to laugh and continued until his rapid pulse eased. *How do I have a pulse?* he wondered.

By paying closer attention to his heartbeat, he remembered that he was still alive — in a curse-induced coma, but alive. So, he did have a heart beating in his chest, and that apparently connected with his ghost version. Max's thoughts leaped around from the metaphysical idea of astroprojection to his experiences with Drummond's limits to wondering if different planes of existence had different physics.

He chuckled at this last thought. *I'm floating in an elevator shaft. Of course, physics is different.* Which meant that he could behave differently as well. He needed to sit down with Drummond and learn the basics, but since his ghost partner was unavailable at the moment, Max decided the best thing to do would be to experiment.

Since motions with his arms and legs had already failed, he tried to use force of willpower. He thought about moving toward the doors. Still nothing.

Well, how did I get here? I walked. Max wondered if it could be that simple. He had walked the halls without a thought. Why should he think about it? He'd been walking since he was one year old. Perhaps, if he trusted his ghost body and his natural instincts, the rest would follow.

Max closed his eyes, took a breath, and then simply walked back onto the floor. No problem. He then pictured how Drummond could float around the room and pass through walls.

Putting his arms in front like a flying superhero, he pushed off the ground. And he floated. Not high, not far, but he did not touch the floor, and he did not fall. If he had to be a prisoner of this hospital, at least he got to have this bit of fun.

Except Cecily Hull was nothing fun. He lowered back to the floor and attempted to continue lowering *through* the floor. His body dropped down without any resistance. He did not move fast, but he did move.

By the time he reached the main level, he expected Cecily to be long gone. However, he found her sitting in a sunlit hall connecting the main entrance with the visitor parking garage. Darker wood panels made a curved wall with large windows. Inside was a conference hall. At the far end, just before the sliding doors to the garage, stood a Starbucks kiosk.

As the barista served coffee and sweets to a line of waiting customers, Max noticed that he could not smell the enticing aromas. Drummond had often complained about being unable to enjoy the smell and taste of food. It was like watching a movie instead of actually being right there. It put a distance between Max and the solid world around him.

He hunched his shoulders and looked away. *I really am a ghost.* Not that he had doubted it before, but the reality of his situation plowed into him.

Before he could spiral into a series of depressing thoughts, he saw Cecily Hull pull out a cell phone and make a call. Though he could not smell coffee, he could hear people speak, and right then, Max figured no conversation could have been more important to listen to. He drifted towards her, ignoring the watchful glares of three women who, by their dress, died sometime in the 1960s.

"Well?" she said as a form of greeting.

Max leaned in to hear the voice on the other end, but Cecily kept her phone pressed tight against her ear.

"That's not good enough." She crossed her legs as if swatting off flies with her feet. "I need more than accusations ... I know it's true but I need proof, and the only one who could provide that is Devan." Her lips twisted down as she listened to the response. "I don't care ... Then you tell him that either he finds Devan or he finds the fastest route out of North Carolina, and that goes for you, too ... Look here, Mr. Pescatore, I have been pleased with the work you have done so far. I know your ambitions and you know mine. If you want to be positioned to benefit from my rise, then you must be willing to get involved in all aspects of my work. Sometimes that gets messy. You understand? This family has been mired in dark swamps of sin for a long time. If I am to bring us into the twenty-first century, it means that none of us can afford to act as if we're above the stench. Not yet, at least." Her lips twitched upward but the rest of her face remained stoic. "That's a much better response. Go to work now. I look forward to hearing of your success."

As she placed the phone into her purse, Max heard Sandra's voice. "What are you doing down here?"

She had spoken to Max, but Cecily answered, "I've been waiting for you."

Sandra glanced down at Cecily. "Ms. Hull? What's going on here?"

Max went over to give Sandra a kiss, almost touched her, before he remembered he was a ghost and contact would only cause her pain. "This shouldn't surprise you. I'm cursed and the Hull family shows up."

"Please, Mrs. Porter, I come on urgent business."

"No," Sandra said. "My husband is in a coma. I have no interest in hearing about your problems."

"You know better than that. From the very start, your husband's actions tied our families together. He threatened to expose some of our darker secrets should anything happened to him."

"That was years ago, and since Tucker's return, it seems the journal is of no value now."

"Let's not verbally gamble when we both know I hold the stronger hand. The journal always has value. And as such, if the Hulls have a problem, then so do the Porters. We are tied together. So, may I come up to the room with you, so we can talk?"

Though her muscles stiffened, Sandra said, "You can go wherever you want." She thought for a second. "What is it you *do* want anyway?"

"I thought that was obvious. I want to hire you."

Chapter 5

RISING THROUGH CEILING AFTER CEILING, Max had time to worry. He wanted to zip back to his room, but flying upward took more effort than dropping down. By the time he joined Sandra and Cecily, the two women had seated near his comatose body, steady glares firing between them. Max wanted to ask Sandra what had happened, but he knew to stay quiet. Drummond had taught him long ago that listening often produced better answers.

Cecily tugged on her silk blouse and straightened her shoulders. "I shouldn't have expected more cordial behavior. After all, money does not give one manners."

"That explains you a whole lot better."

"Careful, Mrs. Porter. I'm willing to trade barbs because I want your services. But don't think you are irreplaceable. Continue to be this rude to me, and I will make sure you regret it."

Max floated behind Cecily, but before he could open his mouth, Sandra threw a venom-filled look at him. He ran his fingers across his lips, zipping them up, and then mimed tossing away the key.

To Cecily, Sandra said, "You'll have to forgive me, but our dealings with the Hull family have never gone smoothly, and on top of that, my husband is right here in bad shape."

"Apology accepted. I, too, am under a great strain, so if I'm a little curt, you'll understand why."

"Jeez," Max said. "If that's true, she's been under a strain since the day we met her." Max waved off Sandra's glare and made another lip-zipping motion.

Sandra said, "Please, Ms. Hull, tell me what you want to hire our little firm to do."

Cecily rubbed her palm against her side. Her fingers looked bony and sharp. Though she could not see Max, she appeared to react to him anyway, snapping her hand back to her lap, then lacing her fingers tight to keep her hands still.

"The Magi Group," she said with a bitter snarl. "They are moving against Tucker. I want you to help me stop them."

"You want to stop the Magi from taking down Tucker Hull — the man you are actively trying to take down. Why? You could have them do all the work for you."

"And what happens then? The Magi Group is every bit as twisted and corrupt as Tucker has made the Hull family business. Right now, the two organizations keep each other in a balanced state. With the Magi Group striking at the Hulls, you're about to see the equivalent of a gang war. There won't be drive-by shootings, but there will be plenty of bodies — many of them cursed into eternities of hellish suffering. But I won't insult you by pretending to care about people. The fact remains that if the Magi Group succeeds, they'll be too powerful for me to fight, and we'll all be living under the thumb of Mother Hope."

Max tried to hold his tongue, but he blurted out, "It's worse than that for her. If Mother Hope wins, she'll have decimated the Hulls, leaving nothing worth having for Cecily."

Sandra kept her eyes on Cecily. "Of course, if Tucker Hull fights off the Magi Group, then you have an even stronger foe in him. In order for you to win in any of this, you have to get them to find a balance again, if not a temporary peace."

"Tucker is steeped in using dark magic, and Mother Hope is a witch. I, however, am neither. Which is why I need your help, and I can see that you have always been the real brains of your operation."

"Flattery, now?"

"Not at all. I'm merely acknowledging the state of your business."

Max stepped between the two women. "Get rid of her.

We're already screwed up enough with Mother Hope. You cannot seriously be thinking about whatever she's going to ask of you. Not to mention, she's a Hull."

Sandra leaned back. "Are you comfortable enough here? We could always finish this conversation at a diner or something?"

"Okay, okay," Max said. "I'll shut up."

Crossing her arms, Cecily gazed off to the side. "I hardly think a diner would be appropriate. Besides, I should hope we are nearly done."

"Fine," Sandra said, also crossing her arms. "Perhaps you could tell me how I'm going to help you stop a war between the Magi Group and the Hull family."

"Research, of course. That's what you people are good at, right? I would have preferred your husband for this, but you'll do."

"Gee, thanks for the vote of confidence."

"This whole thing has been brewing for a long time. I had hoped it would blow over and tensions would settle, but Tucker keeps trying to gain more and more power — mostly of the magic variety. Yet despite all he's acquired, he has not done anything with it. Small things, sure, but nothing significant. He's even allowed you to remain. I think the Magi Group smells the weakness. Or perhaps they feared if they didn't act now, he might strike harder than they were prepared for. Whatever the case, over the last few months, I knew things had taken an ugly turn. So, I employed a woman who knew her way with computers and had her access the Hull family archives."

"You hired a hacker to hack your own family?"

"They hate me. I'm not even allowed in the main house."

Max huffed. "I hate her, too."

With a sharp sniff, Cecily continued, "We were able to pull up Mother Hope's file. Yes, we have files on everybody we deal with — including you. Unfortunately, the Hull computers are well maintained when it comes to security. Before we could download the files, a countermeasure destroyed our computers — I believe my employee said we had been *fried*. I did, however, get a glimpse of the file and I wrote down a code —

ZSRLH. I think it's important."

Sandra bit the inside of her cheek. "Those letters could be nothing more than a filing notation. There's no reason to think it's tied to anything of value."

"I thought so, too. But when I started inquiring for further information, I was shut down. Everybody I contacted about that code stalled or disappeared or, in one case, outright refused to answer. Family that talks to me, employees who have been working for us for years, anybody connected with our archives — not a single person was willing to discuss this with me. Those letters mean something. And they're the only thing I have."

"Okay," Sandra said, typing the letters into her phone. "I'll look into it."

"Thank you. Naturally, this must become your highest priority. I don't know how long we have until Mother Hope or Tucker Hull makes a big move."

"My fee will have to be higher, considering the time constraints."

"Of course."

Cecily offered her hand. Sandra gave a firm shake and watched Cecily walk out. Over her shoulder, Cecily said, "You best get to work right away. Oh, and sorry about your husband."

Max followed Cecily into the hall. As she walked toward the elevators, he caught sight of Dr. Fremont — the high-heeled spy. Fremont pretended to be studying a medical chart until Cecily left the floor. Then she pulled out her cell and made a call.

Returning to his room, Max found Sandra sitting on the bed and holding his body's hand. Then she turned to the ghost-Max. "She's lucky I didn't strangle her."

Max ran his fingers along the back of his neck. "Why are you agreeing to work with her in the first place? Especially when you know the situation I'm in. If Mother Hope finds out, I'm screwed."

Sandra straightened the blanket on Max's body and tucked

him in tight. "Your faith in me is overwhelming."

"I'm not trying to doubt you."

"But you do anyway. After all we've been through."

"Please don't pick a fight. Not now. I am on your side. I believe in you."

"You don't show it. Even before all this — at the party. Maybe even before that. What's going on? We're supposed to be open with each other."

Max struggled for the words. He thought about the money troubles looming on the horizon or the way a marriage ebbs and flows or how risking the lives of those he loves had become normal. "I think it's the lack of control. Not that I have to be in charge of everything, but right now — especially right now — I have zero control over my life."

Sandra offered a sympathetic grin. "You're a very silly man. Don't you know why our marriage works? It's because life always flies out of control, but we're there for each other. Right now, I'm here to pick up the pieces for you. As long as you need me to, I'm here. You'd do the same for me."

"Okay," Max said. He always felt better when they talked out a problem — even if they didn't arrive at a solution.

Sandra kissed Max's forehead before looking at the ghost version. "You better calm down. Just because you're not fully dead doesn't mean you're immune to the properties of being a ghost."

Max recalled the time Drummond's high emotional stress had nearly turned him into the kind of ghost that haunts and destroys. "Can that really happen to me?"

"I don't know. I've never dealt with one like you before."

"You do see us all, don't you?" He thought of the hospital hallway. "How can you stand to be in this place?"

"My husband is lying here in a coma. Where else am I going to be?"

"But, honey —"

"I'll be fine. Let's just get you back in the land of the living."

His chest swelled. "You're incredible."

"Don't start getting all romantic. You're a ghost and that's only cool if you're Demi Moore." She blushed anyway.

Max did his best Drummond clap. "Okay, then. Let me in on why we agreed to be hired by both sides of this fight?"

"First off, we didn't. We agreed to work for Cecily Hull, not the Hull family. And we never agreed to work for the Magi Group. We were coerced into that."

"Isn't that semantics?"

"Maybe. But if we don't keep this clear, it's going to get confusing. The whole point is for us to have the clearest picture — better than the Magi Group, better than Cecily, and most certainly, better than Tucker Hull."

Max nodded. "And what better way to see the big picture than to have Cecily and Mother Hope feeding us information."

"Exactly. We play on both of these teams until we can see the true situation. Then we decide how it all ends."

"Like I said before — you're incredible. Playing both sides against each other."

"Let's just hope we don't get crushed in the middle."

Chapter 6

THE DIGITAL CLOCK ON HIS HEART MONITOR read 2:37 am. Max stared at it until it changed to 2:38. The television flickered images of one enthusiastic salesman after another, each getting their allotted time to infomercial their way to riches. Sandra had fallen asleep in her chair with a book on witches open in her lap. She heard none of it.

Not so for Max. *No need for sleep* turned out to be one of the side effects of being a ghost. His mind didn't understand, though. He saw the night sky, heard the quiet tones, and his mind told him it was time to go to bed. His ghost form, however, felt nothing — no tired bones or muscles, no heavy eyelids, no weariness of any kind. He was wide awake.

No wonder so many ghosts act the way they do. They're bored out of their minds.

Earlier, he had wearied his brain, thumbing over the code Cecily had provided: ZSRLH. He tried simple substitution which brought no sensible results. He considered it as a jumble, but it lacked vowels. He wracked his brain for some historical event that the letters might stand for or some long forgotten acronym. Nothing made sense.

2:39 am. He considered tackling the code again, but codes were not his strength. That belonged to the puzzle-fiend he had married. Still, there were only five letters. How complicated could a code be with only five letters?

The clock changed over another minute. Max turned away. He drifted through the door and into the hall. *Might as well haunt the hospital with everyone else.*

With the living all comfy and asleep, the hallways were much easier to negotiate. Though still crowded with ghosts, their presence did not crowd Max's sense of space in the same way.

"Or maybe I'm just getting used to it," he said.

He dropped through the floor a few times until he saw the ghost of a young man staring out a window. The man wore a tuxedo with a top hat as though he starred in some old Hollywood musical. At any moment, Fred Astaire would come tap dancing across the tiled floor.

Max slid up next to the young man. He tipped his hat towards Max.

"How long you been dead?" Max asked.

The ghost remained silent.

"Sorry. Is that a bad thing to ask? I'm new to all this."

The ghost stared at him but said nothing.

"You got a name or anything?"

The ghost's brow pulled in tight.

It reminded Max of how frustrated Drummond had been when they first met. Back then, Drummond had been bound to his old office by a curse. He tried to communicate with the ghosts that came near, but few would acknowledge him and fewer would talk. Conversations were difficult.

And now I'm cursed. Max wondered if perhaps the dead had trouble hearing him. Probably. Not only was Max cursed, but he still had a foot in the living. However, Max knew that it was more than difficulty with communications. It was the curse. Ghosts did not like to deal with cursed ghosts. They feared they would be caught under the spell as well.

"Thanks for your time," Max said with a slight bow. The young man bowed and tipped his hat again, slowly returning to his vigil at the window.

As Max walked away, he thought more about Drummond. Particularly, he wondered why Drummond had yet to return. He was simply going to put out a few feelers, try to get the groundwork laid to find Dr. Connor. Max needed his old friend back. He had a thousand questions about a being a ghost and Drummond was his one surefire source.

Probably why he's taking a long time.

Dropping a few more floors, Max worked his way to the cafeteria. It was a nice set up — bright and clean with hardwood floors and plenty of open space. Even with all the ghosts, the area felt uncluttered. Four cash registers had been set up like little islands while all the food stations were along the perimeter like a mall food court. This late at night, a single cashier sat at the ready while half the food stations were closed.

On one wall was a freezer with *HERSHEY'S ICE CREAM* pasted on the side. Max looked down through the freezer's glass top. It had been years since he had tasted a chocolate eclair or a strawberry shortcake bar. If only he could reach in and scoop up some of those ice cream treats.

"You can't do that," the cashier said.

Max jerked to the side and looked over at the cashier. "You can see me?"

But she wasn't looking at him. Her eyes were on the man walking in through the side door clearly marked EXIT — a pale-skinned man with a long scar from the corner of his eye down to his jaw. The pale man grinned at the cashier, a grin Max had seen right before being run off the road and into a tree. Though he knew it was all in his mind, Max thought he felt his mouth go dry.

As the pale man walked by her, the cashier took a sudden interest in cleaning her station. He never took his eyes away, as if daring her to look up. When he finally headed down the hall, she shook her head and said to a busboy, "They don't pay me enough to have to worry about people breaking in here through that stupid door."

"Yeah," said the busboy. "How long have we been asking them to fix that? And still nothing."

She went on listing her complaints, but Max no longer listened. The possibility that the pale man had come to the hospital to visit a friend was not a possibility at all. The only reason he could have come, especially at almost three in the morning, was to finish the job.

Sandra was in trouble.

Max jumped into the air and continued upward. As he

passed up through floor after floor, he stretched his neck and arms ahead, trying to quicken his ascent. The pale man had avoided the main lobby because he was avoiding being seen by too many people and cameras. *That's good*, Max thought. It meant that there was a strong chance the pale man would opt for the stairwell instead of the elevator.

Another floor drifted by. Two more to go.

"One of you ghosts, go wake my wife!" Max had no belief any of the ghosts would hear him or comply, but it felt good to shout. Maybe Sandra would hear.

When he finally reached his floor, an elevator dinged. Max watched the metallic doors slide open, holding his breath the entire time. A nurse stepped off and quietly headed to the main desk. No pale man. That was a good sign. He must have taken the stairs — unless he was already in the room.

Max zipped through the hall, bumping aside ghosts, and burst in the room. Sandra sat in the same chair, her eyes closed, a soft snore escaping her lips.

"Wake up!"

She startled and her book flopped off her lap. She launched across the room to Max's body. "What is it? What's wrong?" she said as she looked over him and checked the heart monitor and IV.

"My body's fine. But the guy who ran us off the road is here — the Pale Man." As fast as possible, Max explained what he had seen. "You've got to get out of here."

"What about you?"

"I'm a ghost. He can't even see me."

"I mean your body. What if he's come to finish you?"

"Why would Mother Hope go to the trouble of cursing me and talking to us about finding Dr. Connor and all of that, if she was just going to send somebody to kill me?"

"But maybe she —"

"No time for this. He'll be here any moment."

"I can't leave you vulnerable."

"Come on," Max said, wishing he could slam his hand on a

table or a wall. "Across the hall. That room's empty. Go in there now. I'll stay here, and if there's a problem for my body, I'll yell for you."

Sandra hesitated but finally nodded and dashed across the hall. Max watched her until the door closed. Then he stood by his body.

Moments later, the Pale Man entered the room. His head turned slowly as he scanned across the bed, the chairs, and to the bathroom. He pulled out a large hunting knife.

"Mrs. Porter," he whispered. "You in there?"

He ducked his head into the bathroom and pulled back fast. When nothing jumped him, he flicked the light on and pulled back the shower curtain. He returned, moving faster now, and crossed over to the window. He leaned his head against his arm and his arm against the glass.

Max shot over to Sandra. "He's here for you. He knows you're not in there and he did nothing to my body. You've got to move now."

"Okay," she said, nodding her head over and over. "Okay."

"It'll be fine. Just hold on." Max stuck his head through the wall to look up and down the hall. "All clear. Go for the elevators."

Sandra closed her eyes, breathed in, and counted to three. She opened the door and walked the hall. Max followed. She pressed the call button and kept her body facing the elevator doors. Her fingers tapped against her leg.

As the doors slid open, Max saw the Pale Man leave his room. "Go, go. Hurry."

Sandra jumped into the elevator, pressed 'L', and thumbed the *Close Door* button over and over. The Pale Man hustled toward her. As the doors slid closed, he turned for the stairs. But a second elevator opened and a doctor exited. The Pale Man rushed in and headed down.

Max dropped through the floors. He tried to slow his short, quick breaths, tried to focus on descending faster, but he had a long way to go before he had mastered moving as a ghost. By the time he reached the bottom, the Pale Man already stood in a corner of the lobby, looking all around.

Max liked that — the Pale Man was still afraid to be too public. That might help Sandra. Max floated right by and toward the visitor's garage. He found Sandra near the Starbucks kiosk (closed for the night). She had stopped at a wall that turned toward the sliding glass doors leading into the garage.

Spotting Max, she said, "Two men are down there."

Max nodded and flew into the garage. One glance and he knew the two men were trouble. They wore dark clothing, and both had hunting knives strapped to their sides.

"Can't go that way," he said to Sandra when he returned.

"Where then?"

He went back toward the lobby but drifted across the glass wall of the convention hall. He came up to the door and noticed it had a push bar. Sandra stood on the other side.

Wincing as he reached forward, he pushed against the bar. But his hand slipped right through. He tried again.

"Max," Sandra said, the worry in her voice palpable. She looked toward the lobby, and Max didn't have to see to know — the Pale Man was coming.

He stared at the push bar and tried again. He slipped through once more. *Stop trying so hard,* he reminded himself. Floating, going through walls, all the movement he had done so far had been easy enough when he simply did it without thinking. The harder he attempted to do something, the harder it became to do.

He glanced up at Sandra. She looked back, her eyes unblinking. *I just want to let my wife join me. That's all. She's on the other side of a door, and I just have to open it.*

He pushed the bar, and it depressed. A smile rose on his mouth for a fraction of a second. Then his hand started to burn as if touching a hot stove. He pulled back and the pain disappeared. But he had opened the door enough.

Sandra yanked to door fully open, dashed in, and brought it closed behind her. As she bolted blindly down the convention hall lobby, Max saw the Pale Man rattling the door. It wouldn't stop him for long.

The lobby had a few upholstered chairs on a carpeted side and a long stretch of stone tiles on the other side. On the tiled side, the title VOLUNTEER HALL hung above wood double doors. At the far end, Sandra whipped open a door that led to an off-white hall of offices. She rushed on down with Max close behind. She turned right at one corner, left at another.

Max noticed an open door with a keypad up ahead. "There," he said.

They jumped in, pulling the door shut behind. Sandra bent over with her hands on her knees and coughed. As she caught her breath, Max checked out where they were — part of a kitchen, apparently.

Two enormous walk-in freezers took up one wall. Standard industrial kitchen shelving was everywhere, gleaming metal and stacked with coffee urns, serving trays, plates and bowls, and lots of flatware.

"You gotta keep moving," Max said.

"Go check."

Max passed through the wall and back up the way they had come. The Pale Man had managed to break into the convention area and was wandering the office halls. Max shot back to Sandra.

"He's coming."

She nodded and started deeper into the kitchen. They went out a back door which led to a long stretch of loading docks — all closed for the night. Thick pipes travelled overhead while empty wooden pallets had been stacked in neat piles on a smooth, concrete floor. At one point, they found an upright piano against a wall. Max stopped to look at it, confused by its appearance.

Sandra kept walking. Over her shoulder, she said, "Yeah, honey, it's weird. Let's stay focused."

Max came up beside her. From the loading docks, they entered another off-white hall. A sign read ENVIRONMENTAL SERVICES. "What's that mean?"

"I think it's janitors and such."

Down one hall, up another, right turns, left turns. The

underbelly of the hospital proved to be a confusing maze. As they entered a section which turned out to be the real kitchen — the previous kitchen proved to be more of staging area for the conventions — Max wondered how anybody got fed at all. Those serving food to patients could take a wrong turn and never been seen again.

Room after room of the kitchen looked like an industrial shop — thin walls with notice boards, brown-tiled floors, massive ovens, and metal refrigerators everywhere. Rooms storing boxes of food from floor to ceiling matched rooms filled with rolling carts for tray upon tray of meals. As Sandra hurried steadily along, she saw nobody working — it was three in the morning, after all.

A commotion from behind echoed toward them. "Keep going," Max said as he zipped back toward the noise. The Pale Man worked his way towards them, stopping to check every door and peer around each corner. Moving through the kitchen, Max spotted only two staff working. Somebody in charge would be coming along any moment, but the Pale Man showed no fear of that.

He paused as something caught his attention. A voice — "You ain't supposed to be back here. You lost?" Somebody talking to Sandra. As the Pale Man pulled out his hunting knife and jogged towards the voice, Max soared back to his wife.

"Hide," he said.

Sandra dashed off, moving faster through the endless kitchen.

"Hey!" The kitchen worker shook his head as he went to a phone. "I'm calling security on you."

Max knew Sandra wanted to run, but speeding through a kitchen with hot food and wet floors was asking for a twisted ankle or a broken bone or worse. Max flew through walls, checking out every side room. Lots of storage for produce and canned goods, but each of these rooms had no escape route, and with the Pale Man closing in and, presumably, security on its way soon, she had to find an escape.

Turning a corner, she passed four large vats for soup. Steam came out of two of them, but one was cold and empty.

"In there," Max said.

Sandra hesitated.

"Everywhere I look is a dead end or too open to hide."

The sound of running feet changed her mind. With her jaw shivering from a cocktail equal parts adrenaline and fear, she winced as she swung a leg over the lip of the vat. She lowered down and closed the top.

"Don't worry," Max said — not for Sandra's sake, but his own.

The Pale Man entered the soup room. He jogged right by into the next section. Seconds later he returned. Holding his knife at the ready, he scanned the room. He crouched low and searched for signs of Sandra hiding behind a counter.

"He's here," Max told Sandra. "Keep still."

The Pale Man narrowed his eyes upon the soup vats. He glanced at the two hot vats first as he walked toward the cold ones. The one Sandra had not jumped in still had its top open. Max swore — he should have thought about that.

Wetting his lips, the Pale Man leaned over the closed vat. With the hilt of his knife, he banged on the top. "Mrs. Porter," he said with a gentle Carolina accent, "I know you're in there. Come on out, now. I just have a few questions is all. Nothing to be so scared about."

Nothing. Not a sound.

The Pale Man put his ear to the vat. "Mrs. Porter? You in there?"

Max suspected what Sandra planned and he knew exactly how to help. "Now, honey!"

Sandra shoved the lid open, smashing the Pale Man's jaw and cheek while throwing him backward. As she climbed out of the vat, the man tried to stand firm, but he stumbled and fell to one knee. Blood dribbled down his cheek.

"That wasn't very nice," he said. Groaning, he dug his fingers into his mouth and yanked out a tooth. "Not nice at all."

He stood in Sandra's way. Max cheered as she punched the

Pale Man and dashed by him. But despite his injuries, the man moved quickly.

His hand snapped out and grabbed Sandra's arm. He spun her in and pressed his knife against her throat. "Now, you're going to answer me one simple question. You answer honestly, you live. Stall or lie or anything, and I slit your throat. Understand?"

Sandra nodded, though her eyes were on Max. He tried to comprehend her look — more than simple fear, she seemed to be trying to communicate something to him.

"Good," the Pale Man said. "My employer simply wants to know if Max Porter is a ghost. I'm assuming you understand whatever that means. Doesn't really matter to me. But that's the question I want answered — is Max Porter a ghost?"

"He is," she said. "And he can do all the things a ghost can do."

"What's that mean?"

Max understood. He flew in close and thrust his hand into the Pale Man's head. The pain of touching a living being hit as if Max's skin were made of glass and somebody had thrown a rock right through, shattering him into pieces. He screamed right along with the Pale Man.

Sandra had no trouble extricating herself from the man's shivering body. "I'm free," she said, and Max released his victim. The Pale Man crumpled to the floor, panting hard and convulsing in short bursts.

"In here," the kitchen worker called out from nearby.

Sandra turned to Max. "I've got to get moving. Meet me in your room." She paused long enough to give Max a shudder — he knew her looks so well, and to see the one he loved most, the one that said they were always for each other, thrilled him.

"Go," he said, holding his hand close to his chest. "I'll be up once the pain stops blinding me."

Sandra looked as if she might try to kiss him, but the jangle of a police belt woke her back to her situation. She walked off in the opposite direction. Moments later, a security officer entered the room with one of the kitchen staff leading the way.

The officer moved quickly to disarm the Pale Man — not too difficult considering the rough shape he was in — and slapped cuffs on him before the man could utter a sound.

Max waited a few minutes until he knew for sure that the Pale Man wouldn't get loose and come after Sandra. Once two other security officers entered the kitchen and talked of how long they'd have to wait until the police showed up, Max thought he could safely leave. He floated up through the floors and down the halls until he reached his room.

When he entered, he found Sandra sitting next to the bed, clutching his body's hand. Across the room sat a man dressed in a white-and-gray striped suit and holding a porkpie hat in his hand. Seeing Max, he jumped to his feet and walked over with his hand extended.

"Ah, Mr. Porter, delighted to meet you."

Max shook the ghost's hand even as he looked at Sandra for some explanation. She shrugged, and the strain of the night played out in her trembling shoulders.

"Who are you?" Max asked.

"Oh, yes, forgive me. My name is Corenlius Pendingworth. I'm an attorney for Mr. Tucker Hull."

Chapter 7

"WELL, MR. PENDINGWORTH, we've had a long, difficult day and an even longer, more difficult night. There's nothing you have to say that can't wait a few hours. So, you best leave right now and allow my wife some rest."

Mr. Pendingworth rolled his fingers along the rim of his hat. "I'm sorry, truly am, but I cannot do that. Mr. Hull left specific instructions, and well, I know you both are well aware of what it is like to deal with the Hull family and their instructions."

Though her fingers shook, Sandra gestured to the chair. "Get it over with, please."

"Yes. Certainly. Well, you see, Mr. Hull wants me to inform you that it has come to his attention that you are possibly working for a woman who goes by the name of Mother Hope. Now, while it is true that you are no longer under the employment of the Hull family, it is equally true that Mr. Hull would not want you being employed by a group sworn to undermine anything he attempts to accomplish. So, with that laid out and in mind, my client wants you to cease and desist all actions taken on the part of the Magi Group and/or Mother Hope. Failure to comply will be met with swift justice."

Max rubbed the bridge of his nose. "When are you from?"

"Excuse me?"

"You're not an idiot. When are you from?"

Mr. Pendingworth glanced about the room as if searching for a hidden film crew. "I was born in 1802 and died in 1827."

"How'd you die?"

"That's rather personal."

"Fine. Then go tell Mr. Hull that I don't take you seriously."

"Of course you do. I can see on your face that you are frightened of my every word. I, on the other hand, am utterly calm."

Drummond appeared standing next to the attorney. "Perhaps I can change that."

The attorney's face fell. "Oh. Mr. Drummond. I didn't realize you were, that is to say, I was uninformed regarding the relationship these individuals had with you, and —"

"Just answer his question. How'd you die?"

"Something spooked my horse. It threw me off, and before I knew what had happened it stomped me. Broke a few ribs. I thought that was all, but in the end, the bones had done far worse damage inside my body. I died slowly and in a lot of pain."

"And?"

"And what?"

Drummond grabbed the ghost and threw him against the wall. "And you best finish the story and get the hell out of here. I've had long day and a longer night, and I'm sick of dealing with ghosts that won't talk with me."

Max smiled at Drummond's choice of words. Mr. Pendingworth sputtered. "Well, I simply meant to say that later, after my death, I found I was unable to move on. My death was no accident. Mr. Hull wanted to have representation in the ghost realm, so he had my demise arranged. Shall I go now?"

"Don't come back."

"Good evening, gentlemen." Mr. Pendingworth scuttled off through a wall.

Max chuckled. "Thanks."

Drummond took off his hat. "We're partners. We look out for each other."

"Could've used your help a little bit ago," Sandra said. Her voice sounded sturdy and the tremors in her hands had gone. She quickly told Drummond about her unintended exploration of the hospital kitchens.

"That doesn't make much sense. Why would Mother Hope send this guy after you twice? Especially when she succeeded in her goal the first time. She got Max vulnerable enough to curse. So why come after you?"

"Haven't a clue."

Max said, "Hon, I wasn't lying when I told that lawyer you needed to sleep. Shove my body aside and get some rest. This was only the first full day of this case."

"Not really a case," Drummond said.

"Whatever it is, it's been an exhausting day for us. If I wasn't a ghost, I'd be half asleep already."

"There aren't many benefits to being dead, but I suppose that's one of them."

"Yeah. I tried that touching humans thing. Not a benefit by far."

Drummond's eyebrows lifted high. "I'm impressed. That's a tough thing to endure."

"Didn't really have a choice." Max stopped. A soft snoring rustled the air as Sandra's head had drooped over Max's body. "That doesn't look comfortable."

"I'm sure you can wake her, and she'll shift over to something better."

"Let her sleep. She's had enough interruptions. Besides, both of us can stand guard. Don't have to worry about another hitman coming in."

Drummond scratched his chin and set his hat back on at an angle. "You sure that was a hitman?"

"You don't think so?"

"If we accept Mother Hope's version of it, then she hired this man to send you to the hospital, not the morgue. In fact, it sounded to me like she was a bit miffed about the job he did. She seemed to think he went too far. He nearly did kill you, after all."

Max gazed upon his slumbering body. "Then they send the same guy again?"

"That's my point. If this guy was good at his job — I mean good for a group like the Magi — then he wouldn't dream of doing anything but exactly what he was ordered to do. Everything I'm hearing about him suggests he's a freelancer.

So, either Mother Hope is lying — and in this case, I don't see the advantage for her to do that — or somebody else hired him."

Max folded his arms. "It was Tucker."

"Don't go assuming. We know Tucker sent the lawyer, but—"

"It was Tucker. I didn't think about it before, but at one point the hitman said *my employer.* Just like Mr. Modesto."

"Except why would Tucker Hull send a hitman after Sandra to ask if you were a ghost when he's got a ghost lawyer who can affirm that fact right now?"

"Well, who else could it be? Who needs to know if I'm part-ghost?"

"I'm not sure, but I don't like it."

Max checked the clock — 5:21 am. He hoped Sandra would be allowed to sleep until noon because the more he learned, the more he thought things were going to get much worse. She would need to be in top form as soon as possible.

"We've got a lot of time to wait here, and I don't think we'll find an answer to the hitman question soon," Max said, positioning himself so that he had a clear view of the door. "So, what did you find out in the Other? Any leads on Dr. Connor?"

"Oh, I found her."

Max jolted upright. "What? Why didn't you say anything?"

"Ease back, pal. Your hitman situation took priority."

"Like hell. I can't get out of this mess without Dr. Connor."

"Which is why you won't like what I have to say. So, trust your partner and relax. There's nothing to do this very second."

"But where is she? I don't see her."

"She's not here. I got Leed watching her."

"Leed? What can a blob of light do?"

"Do you want to hear this or should I go for a walk?"

Rolling his head back, Max dropped his arms. "Just tell me what happened."

"Thank you. Now, when I started out, I thought it was going to be a tough grind, but I've taught you the importance of building a network of contacts and informants. Turns out, they had the answers for me right away. Apparently, Dr. Connor is something of a celebrity, a real sight-seeing stop for ghosts."

"For my own sanity, I'll ignore the idea of ghosts on vacation, but why is she a celebrity?"

Drummond pointed at Max and winked. "You keep getting better and better at the detective racket. You're really starting to zero in on the key questions."

"Thanks. What's the answer?"

"I'm coming to that, and brace yourself because you are not going to like this."

"I already don't like it."

"Good, then you'll be prepared. Dr. Connor has a rare and unique curse on her."

"You're joking."

"Nope. Looks like there's a lot of it going around."

Max checked his body, then the door. "So, what is it? Can't be what they did to me. We saw her body. She was definitely dead."

"First, she is dead. Don't worry about that. Second, we don't know who cursed her. Might've been Mother Hope, but a witch like Dr. Connor made a lot of enemies in her life — many that would have had the knowledge and capability to pull off this kind of a curse."

"Which is what? What's her curse?"

Drummond leaned back and inspected his shoes. "She's been muted by an iron gag. Didn't even run when she saw me. She's in the worst shape I've ever seen. Even worse than when she was a drunkard who thought everything was lost."

Putting a hand up, Max said, "Hold on. What's an iron gag curse?"

"It's an old way witches were dealt with back in the 1600s. When a village caught a person they thought was a witch, they padlocked a gag made of iron around the mouth — really just a big metal slab crudely shaped to cover the mouth and chin. The idea was that this would stop the witch from uttering a spell before they could sentence her. Then they'd cut her to pieces with a sword."

Max's ghost stomach twisted. "She didn't have an iron gag over her mouth when we found her dead, so you're saying that somebody dug her up and cursed her."

"Exactly. And now she can't speak until the curse is lifted."

"Then she can't work with Mother Hope."

"I think that's the idea. Leed thinks it, too. He'll watch over her, and if something happens, he can pop right into my pocket from the Other and warn us."

Max slashed his hand through the wall. "It's got to be Tucker. All of this."

Over the next hour, the two ghosts debated the idea. Max thought the Pale Man's usage of *my employer* was damning enough, but the muting of Dr. Connor meant that Tucker suspected Mother Hope's plan. If Tucker was finally willing to come after Max and Sandra, then it made sense for him to mute the one witch who could mess things up. Drummond pointed out that they had no real proof of that, but Max countered that argument by saying that if all these clues indicating Tucker were wrong, then the whole thing was one gigantic coincidence.

"And I know what you think of coincidences," Max said.

Drummond did not give in, leaving Max to wonder if his partner was frightened. And that frightened Max more.

As noon arrived, Sandra finally woke. She wasted no time with stretching or rubbing her eyes or even straightening her hair. Instead, she turned to Drummond and said, "Tell me everything."

Drummond told her all that he knew about Dr. Connor, and Max interrupted more times than was required to expound on his ideas and concerns. When their verbal dance finished, Sandra pulled out her cell phone and made a call.

"Leon? This is Sandra Porter. Please inform your boss that we have found Dr. Connor ... That's right. And tell her to come over to the hospital at once ... Well, I don't really care how you phrase it. I just want to make sure she gets over here."

After ending the call, Sandra dropped back into her chair. Max crouched before her. "I don't think you quite heard Drummond," he said.

"I heard him just fine."

"Well, what are you doing then?"

"Hopefully, putting an end to this nonsense. Now, I need to freshen up before they get here." She shuffled off to the bathroom and closed the door. "Don't poke your head in here, either. Just because you're now a ghost doesn't mean I don't get any privacy."

Max looked to Drummond for support, but his partner shrugged. Fifteen minutes later, Sandra returned looking brighter. Her hair no longer shot off at odd directions and the sleepiness in her face had disappeared.

She walked over to Max's body and took his hand. Leaning close, she kissed his cheek. Her lips quivered but she managed to smile.

When she rolled her shoulders back and looked to the door, Max saw her strength return. The thin line she balanced upon had begun to take its toll, but she still has some fight left — probably a lot.

"I'm getting coffee," she said and walked out.

Max gave her a five count to make sure she didn't come back for something. Then he said, "Listen, I was wondering if you could give me a few pointers on this whole ghost business. It took me long enough to figure out how to move, and I can only go up and down floors slowly. You fly around like a jet compared to me."

Drummond pushed his chin toward the door. "Tough dames like that are one in a million."

"Sandra? Don't I know it."

"Also a million times the trouble."

"It's worth it."

Drummond slapped Max in the face. "Then stop asking me crap questions and start working this case. I don't like seeing that look in her eyes. Every single time she even peeks at you lying in that bed, she's picturing you as a corpse. We've got to get you back in that body, not get you comfortable being a ghost."

"Ow. That hurt."

"Good. Slap some sense into you."

Max shoved Drummond back. "I don't *want* to be ghost. I just figured if I'm stuck this way right now, I should be able to get around."

Drummond made a fist. "You could fool me. Send me looking for Dr. Connor, send your wife reading books, what have you done?"

"What can I do?" Max put up his fists, just in case.

"You can think, can't you? You've got a good brain. Start using it. Because I'm telling you now, if you die, I'm going to kill you. No way will I sit around and watch that woman fall apart after you're gone and haunting. I'll rip your ghost-self to shreds."

Sandra entered the room and froze. "What's going on here?"

Both Drummond and Max backed away from each other. "Nothing," Drummond said.

Max put his hands behind his back. "Just discussing the case, and we got a little heated about it."

Setting her coffee aside, Sandra said, "You are both terrible liars. Whatever your problem, put it away right now. There's a window by the vending machines, and I spotted Leon and Mother Hope walking along. They'll be here any minute."

"No problem. Drummond and I both agree that getting this worked out is vital."

"Damn right," she said. "I can't be married to you like this." Max's shocked face brought a smile to her lips. "Really, honey? You think I'm serious?"

Drummond chuckled. "Heck, even I knew she was making a joke."

A minute later, the door opened and Mother Hope entered while Leon stood guard outside. Her eyes had sunken since her last visit, and dark circles had formed beneath them. She wore a plain, gray frock that made her appear smaller and older.

Despite this, when she took a seat, placed her palms on her knees, and cocked her head towards Sandra, everybody in the room knew the old woman still had plenty of power.

Sandra took a sip of coffee, set the cup back down, and crossed her arms casually. She remained standing as she stared back at Mother Hope.

Neither spoke.

Only the steady beeping of Max's heart monitor filled the air.

Mother Hope looked around the room, and Max smiled. It was a slight win in this battle of wills, but the war wouldn't end until one of them talked first. Nothing stopped Max or Drummond from talking, though both stayed quiet as well.

"I don't have time for games," Mother Hope finally said. "I'm here. Report to me."

The corner of Sandra's mouth turned up a sliver. "No reporting going on. I don't work for you."

"You most certainly do."

"Coercion is a different matter than employment. You are not my boss."

"But I do hold your husband's life in my hands. So, can we stop with this power struggle and accept the way things are?"

Sandra pulled over a chair and sat. "Of course. Let's accept the way things are. We have found Dr. Connor, and we can connect you to her. Our end of this is done. Release my husband from this curse. Bring him back to me."

"Well, bless your heart. You think I just fell of the truck? I am not going to simply accept your word for it all. I will free your husband once Dr. Connor has fulfilled her end of the spell."

"There's the problem. Dr. Connor has been cursed as well — an iron gag. We need to locate her corpse and break her from her curse before she can help you. But I can't do that alone. This calls on the research skills Max has always excelled at, and he can't do anything like that in his current state."

Drummond said, "Doll, you never cease to amaze me. Great going!"

"You've got her on the ropes," Max said.

But Mother Hope grinned enough to show her teeth. "This is not a good play for you."

"Oh? Seems like the play is in your hands, not mine. You have a choice to make. If you want to defeat Tucker Hull, you'll need Max to release that witch. You'll have to let him go. Or you can keep him, and Tucker Hull will destroy you."

"No, dear. I've got plenty of qualified people at my disposal. They can find Dr. Connor's gagged corpse. They can break her curse. I don't need your husband for that."

"We've heard that before. Lots of people bet they can beat Max at finding something. He always wins."

"Not this time."

Sandra held her face still, but Max saw the tiny twinge in her cheek. "You're wrong. Regardless, though, the deal was for us to find Dr. Connor, and —"

"Deal? There's no *deal* here. There is only what I want."

"Look, if you —"

Mother Hope hopped to her feet. "You have wasted my time, and I don't have enough of that right now. You want your husband? You know what has to be done. Don't call me here again unless you have success." She whipped her finger at Sandra. "Waste my time again, and I'll curse you far worse than you've ever seen."

After Mother Hope left, nobody spoke. Had he not been a ghost, Max would have put his arm around his wife, but had he not been a ghost, none of this conversation would have happened.

Drummond tilted his hat back. "Well, doll, you sure know how to piss off a witch."

Sandra spun to face him. "I am not laughing."

"Honey," Max said, "he's only trying to —"

"I've had it. All of it. Mother Hope, this curse, every Hull that ever lived and those that are dead, too. I've had it with the witches and the hitman and all the Mr. Modestos and Leons. I've had it with Winston-Salem and North Carolina." She kicked the leg of one chair, tumbling it onto its back.

Drummond went to say something, but Max waved him down. Anything that ghost could say would only be a bellows to the flame.

Max waited until he saw Sandra's fists unclench and her shoulders lower slightly. "You okay?"

"No," she said calmly. She went to Max's body and brushed back his hair. "I can't lose you."

"You're not going to."

"You don't know that."

"I know us. I know we won't stop fighting. My life is hanging in our hands, and if it's going to be that way, then I'm better off here instead of anywhere else."

She sniffled and cracked a smile. "That almost makes sense."

"Then let's work our way through this. We can access the library online from here. You can be my fingers and type what I need, and together we'll get the research going until we can find out what happened to Dr. Connor's corpse."

Sandra perked up. "No," she said. "That's playing right along with what Mother Hope wants us to do. We won't do that."

"We won't?"

Drummond snapped his fingers. "Oh, I like where you're heading."

Max's head turned back and forth between Sandra and Drummond. "What's going on?"

"Your wife is getting back on her feet is what's going on."

As if to illustrate the point, Sandra stood straight and planted her feet down firm. "We do need to find Dr. Connor, but we all know we need Max back here in the flesh in order to succeed. We also know that keeping you as a ghost is Mother Hope's leverage. So, we're going to fix all of that in one strong move." She looked right at Max's ghost. "We'll pull in every favor if we have to, call on everybody we know to help, whatever it takes — we're bringing you back."

Chapter 8

MAX KEPT THINKING about the bottle of whiskey hiding in the bookshelf at the office. The day had moved so slowly that he had wound himself up tight, and a stiff drink would have been relaxing. A little bit, at least.

Sandra and Drummond had left to prepare. Max had asked for details of the plan, but Sandra refused to share. "We're being spied on, hon. They're being obvious about Dr. Fremont watching us. Of course, they'll have other, less obvious surveillance as well."

So, Max had nothing to do but think over all the possible ways the night could derail a plan he knew almost nothing about. He had to remind himself that Sandra was in charge. This was her plan, her preparation, her execution, and while he believed she would do a great job, he did not like being in the dark — especially with his life in the balance and nothing to do but float around the hospital.

After hovering over the nurses as they gave his body a sponge bath and checked his monitors, he knew the excitement of the day had ended. The nurses only came in three times a day — the morning routine, this early afternoon check, and once more in the evening. The day drifted onward.

With nothing to occupy him, Max took another stab at Cecily Hull's code — ZSRLH. Perhaps, instead of a secret code, it was more of an identification code — like a library call number. But what kind of library used five letters like that? He considered that it might be a password to some protected files or a clandestine website, but if that had been true, Tucker Hull would never have written the password down in such an obvious place. Which brought up the possibility that Cecily finding the code was no accident. Perhaps it had been planted for her to find. Except Cecily claimed that she didn't know what the letters meant. Why plant a code for an enemy to find if the enemy couldn't decipher the code?

Long after sunset, after the nurses performed their final duties for the night, he had resigned to another loop of the "aisles of the dead" as he had come to think of his ghostmates in the halls when Sandra entered the room. She set a box down on one chair and pulled out a large container of salt, some chalk, a small mixing bowl, and three candles — two blue, one black.

"No offense," Max said, "but this isn't the kind of magic you can break with a spell learned on a witchcraft website."

Sandra pulled the box apart to reveal a series of symbols drawn on the inside. "Shut up and trust me." She slid the flattened box underneath Max's bed.

Drummond walked in via the outer wall. "All set on my end."

"You're sure about this?" Sandra asked pulling out a piece of paper covered with writing.

"I went over it all twice. Dr. Connor said it's good."

Max grabbed Drummond's arm. "Dr. Connor? She's speaking? What's she doing with this?"

Shrugging free, Drummond said, "She can't talk. But she can write. She gave us this spell. Wrote it down despite the pain, and then I read it back to her. Twice."

"But we can't trust her. She hates me with a passion. A serious burn-me-in-Hell kind of passion."

Sandra said, "We know that, honey."

"Then why —"

"You have got to calm down and remember who you're talking with. I'm not an idiot."

"I'm not trying to second guess you, but —"

"Yes, you are. And I understand that you're worried, that it's your life we're dealing with, that this situation has taken away all choices for you. I also understand something you may not see — that you're not thinking clearly. It's okay. We are. All you have to do is remember this — I love you. Your life is every bit as precious to me, too. And I'm bringing you back."

As Sandra consulted her instructions for the proper placement of the candles — two blues on the floor near the bed's footboard, one black centered underneath the headboard — Drummond took Max aside. "Listen to her. She's giving everything she can for you. We all are. After you're done realizing what a bonehead you're being, start thinking. Obviously, we know the kind of person Dr. Connor is. So why would we trust her even a little bit?"

Max closed his eyes. He tried to wipe away the worry and focus on Dr. Connor. "Because she needs me."

"That's right. For the moment, she's stuck, and she can't get uncursed unless that iron gag is removed."

"She knows we're her best chance."

"Particularly, if we have you at full capacity. So, she helps us. For now."

Pinching the bridge of his nose, Max sighed and approached Sandra. "I'm sorry. I know it doesn't look like it by my behavior, but I do trust you. There's nobody I trust more."

"What else?" Sandra said.

"What do you mean?"

She put her hand on her hip. "What else?"

"I love you."

"Damn right. And you're a dolt, too. Let me hear that."

"And I'm a dolt."

"Okay, sweetheart. On account of extreme stress and being an unwilling ghost, I forgive you."

Drummond flew out through the door and returned a minute later. "The Sandwich Boys are here and in place."

Max grinned. "PB and J are here? What exactly is this plan?"

"Nothing too complicated. In fact, I got this one from you," Sandra said, fishing out her cell phone. "Okay. I think we're about ready to do this."

"Do what? What's going to happen?"

Flexing her fingers, Sandra said, "I told you already. We're getting you back to the living." She typed a text message and sent it off. "Drummond, be a dear and let me know when the Sandwich Boys have started."

"Sure thing. Though I suspect you'll hear it long before I have to tell you."

"Probably, but check anyway."

After Drummond dashed through the wall, Sandra gave the room one final inspection. She checked Dr. Connor's instructions and tapped on the paper as she went through. With a blush, she rushed over to the window and closed the curtains.

From down the hall, Max heard a commotion break out. Jammer J let out a loud whoop as two security guards and a few nurses yelled at him. Thundering boots stomped by the door as either PB or J sprinted by, security in close pursuit.

Drummond returned. "Those boys love it when we tell them to cause a distraction."

"What about Dr. Fremont?"

"Jammer J snatched files right from her hands. She's chasing him harder than security. And she's in high heels, too."

With a nod, Sandra turned away and tapped a few times on her cell phone. "Maria? We're ready."

Minutes later, Maria Cortez-Kane entered the room. She wore robes in various blues and greens like a flowing river, and a headband that matched both in color and flow. She looked like a musical version of a gypsy. Max had only seen her once before at the party she hosted — the same one that ended with him in a coma.

"Her?" Max said, unable to stop himself.

"She's a real witch," Sandra said. "And she's been showing me all about that world. Unless you know of another witch that we can call upon, Maria's our best shot."

Maria waved a hand over Max's body. "I take it the ghost is a bit unsure of me."

"Don't worry about him. He likes to complain. Especially when things are out of his hands."

"Men. Even when they're ghosts, they act the same."

Max smacked his forehead. "I'm right here."

"Ladies," Drummond said, "you don't have a whole lot of time."

Sandra picked up the salt container. "The other ghost wanted to remind us that we are short on time."

"We'll be fine. Let me look over the spell once more."

Sandra handed over Dr. Connor's paper and poured a line of salt across the entranceway. Maria checked over the list, counted candles, inspected Sandra's work on the flattened box, and nodded. She picked up a piece of white chalk and drew a large isosceles triangle that connected the three candles with the two blues at the base and the black candle at the apex.

"Shouldn't that be a circle?" Max said.

Sandra's eyes bulged and her teeth ground tight. Raising his hands, he said, "Okay, I'll shut up. I've just never seen a spell done with a triangle before."

Drummond said, "That's because this isn't a typical spell. Those gals are dealing with a darker level of magic. Circles are used to represent unity and the oneness of the universe and the connection of everything, but triangles are sharp, direct spells. It's the sturdiest geometric shape there is, so it is used to lend power and stability to a difficult spell."

"Look at you. When did you learn so much?"

"Did you already forget our case with the witch coven?"

"Right," Max said, not wanting to dwell on the time Sandra had been possessed by Drummond's ex-girlfriend. "I try to forget that as much as possible."

"Well, you pick up a few things from a relationship like that."

Maria lifted the small mixing bowl that Sandra had brought and carefully walked it over to the side of the bed. "We need to draw his blood."

Drummond smirked. "Told ya. Magic that uses blood and triangles — this is serious stuff."

Despite the growing urge to yell his frustration, Max kept quiet. His experiences with magic told him that this was more than serious — it was deadly. He could urge Sandra not to risk her life, but he knew it would be a waste of their time and energy. She was determined to follow through. After all, that was how they had survived this long. Since he knew he would never convince her to change, the best he could do was stay quiet so that these brave women could focus.

With the sure motions of a trained nurse, Maria pulled the distal port from the IV in Max's arm and placed it in the bowl at his side. She then opened the port, and instead of collecting Max's blood with a syringe, she let it dribble into the bowl. Over her shoulder, she asked Sandra for sterile gauze from the cabinet with all the basic supplies. Once the bottom of the bowl had been painted in a thin layer of thick crimson, Maria wiped the port clean with the gauze and reset Max's IV as if nothing had happened.

"This is it," she said.

Sandra turned to Drummond. "You need to leave."

"Not on your life," Drummond said. "I know I give Max a hard time, but there's no way I'm going to ditch him now."

"I appreciate that. We all do. But Maria has made it clear to me that this spell is unwieldy. I'm not sure how specific we can be in grabbing a ghost. I don't want it grabbing you and putting you into Max's body by accident."

"Ah. That's why you salted the door. Don't want any other ghosts coming in."

"Exactly. So, be the sweet, wonderful ghost I know you are, and please leave. Go help PB and J. I'm sure a few well-timed obstacles will extend their diversion by the few minutes we still need."

"You got it."

"You know where to meet up?"

"Of course. Don't you worry. I'll keep those boys safe." Drummond put his hand out towards Max. "I want to say something. Just in case."

Max smirked. "No need. If something goes wrong, you'll be stuck with me as a ghost forever."

"No. You'll move on. Even if I have to kick you ahead. So, shake my hand." Drummond waited until they shook. Then, he removed his hat and picked at the smooth interior. "You're a good man. You've done right by me more than once. There's no other I'd want at my side when trouble comes." A smile rose on his lips. "Except maybe your wife."

Max tapped Drummond's arm with a fist. "Don't worry. I'm in good hands. Go help the boys."

Placing his hat gently on his head, Drummond dropped through the floor. Sandra returned to Maria. "All clear."

"Turn off the lights," Maria said.

As Sandra hit the wall switch, Maria took a match to the three candles. The flickering wicks created strange shadows that crept out from under the bed and stretched up the walls. Maria directed Sandra to the right side while she stood on the left.

"Have your husband float above his body."

Max did as instructed. "I love you," he whispered to Sandra.

She lifted her head. "No good-byes. I'll see you in a few minutes."

Maria launched into a chant of moans and odd phrases in odder languages. She read straight from Dr. Connor's page, holding it close due to the dim lighting. As she chanted, she handed the bowl of blood to Sandra and indicated for Sandra to hold it between Max's body and his ghost.

The chanting continued, shifting into a steady four-note pattern. Maria took Dr. Connor's paper and held it over a candle. Then she placed the burning page into the bowl. With both hands, she held the bowl, as did Sandra, and together they lifted it higher into the air. Sandra joined Maria in the four-note chant.

Max stared at the small flame in the bowl. It burned steady and clear. Even when the paper had become ash and all that remained was blood, the fire burned. The blood rippled underneath the flame like tiny pebbles being tossed in at odd intervals. Each time, Max felt his skin contract with an involuntary muscle spasm.

His stomach gurgled. He smelled the burning blood. It was sharp and acrid and — Max's eyes widened. He could *smell* the burning.

As if a giant vacuum cleaner had suddenly been switched on,

Max heard a loud whine and felt his head pull towards the bowl. The chanting grew louder. Max's skin tightened even as it stretched downwards. He tried to move with the pull. He tried to go against it. Anything. But his ghost body no longer responded.

The small flame ignited into a blaze. It blinded Max with a bright flash turning everything white and gold.

All faded into darkness.

Max's eyes snapped open. Sandra's bright face floated above him. A tear dropped from her eye onto his cheek. He took a breath and felt air rushing through his nose into his lungs. He forgot how a simple breath could feel so refreshing.

"You did it," he whispered.

Sandra dropped down, snaking her arms around him, and kissed him hard. "Don't ever do that again to me. Understand? No dying."

"I'll do my best."

He heard a short sniffle. Maria stood nearby, dabbing at her eyes with one of her flowing sleeves. "And people say witchcraft is a bad thing. We brought you back together. For love."

Sandra rolled her eyes as she got up. "You're such a softy."

After blowing her nose, Maria said, "Enough reunion. I don't mind things being mushy, but I do mind getting caught here. Let's go. You're welcome to come back to my house. Norman's out of town on business. I've got plenty of room."

Sandra rolled off of Max, putting him and his bed between her and Maria. "I am so sorry. I thought you understood."

With an odd squint, Maria said, "Understood what?"

"You can't go back home. Not yet."

She pulled the flattened box from under the bed and reassembled it. "Oh, please. I hardly think your little boys' escapade is going to cause me any trouble. I mean, it's been fun and all sneaking around, but hardly necessary. My husband has given donations to many medical charities. The hospital would never really do much to me."

Max sat up, surprised that his head didn't ache. "It's not the hospital you have to worry about."

Sandra brought his clothes over. "The people who did this to him are going to be furious when they find out. What did you think happened here?"

"I really didn't consider it," Maria said, still forcing a plastic, hopeful smile as if all of this was a misunderstanding that a few proper phone calls should clear up. "You're a friend, and you asked me to help with a difficult spell. Frankly, I thought it was a fun challenge. I didn't even know if it would work."

"We don't have time for debate. Come with us. We'll explain everything."

"I can't. I have to go home."

As Max slipped on his pants, Sandra walked over and cupped Maria's face. "The people who did this will kill you. Or worse."

Maria's smile faltered.

Chapter 9

BECAUSE HIS ACTUAL INJURIES from the car accident were minor and the source of his coma had been the curse, Max discovered his body felt pretty good — weak from lack of motion for too many days, but good. He had little trouble dressing, and as long as Sandra stood nearby, he thought he could manage a sturdy enough walk that they would avoid notice when leaving the hospital.

Maria no longer spoke more than a few words. Once they were ready to go, she disconnected all of the equipment hooked up to Max and turned it off. At best, nobody would notice for a short time. At worst, alarms would buzz and they would have to improvise a fast escape. The Sandwich Boys saved them.

As Sandra assisted Max out of the room, the alarms at the nurses' station were beeping. However, PB and J's antics (which included toppling several vending machines and turning up the volume on every television they had passed) had caused enough commotion that for a few moments, nobody was paying attention. By the time the nurses rushed into Max's room, Sandra was belting him into the passenger seat of her car.

From Forsyth Medical, they only had a short drive into the city. The night's traffic was light — Max later learned that it was Wednesday night — and they reached Trade Street quickly. Instead of turning towards their office, however, Sandra drove east for a few blocks and parked near an empty lot.

She checked some notes on her cell phone. "PB said to go down this hill to the fence."

With Maria's assistance, Max exited the car, and they all

walked across the lot. Tall grass and thorny weeds brushed against them. Max enjoyed each tiny scratch. Simply being able to feel the real world around him and smell the stale beer cans littering the empty lot curved his mouth upward.

Sandra flicked on a flashlight and led them toward a chain-link fence with barbed wire running along the top. A small section had been cut and bent from repeated use. She held the cut fence back to allow Max and Maria in.

Max turned around and held the other end of fence for Sandra. Then he gazed across the wide expanse leading to an old RJ Reynolds tobacco warehouse. Weeds broke through the faded pavement. Graffiti marred the walls and concrete posts. Many of the windows had been shattered. Two brick smokestacks loomed long shadows over the lot.

Sandra headed toward the nearest building which had an enormous door on one side with train tracks leading up to it. "PB said security rarely bothers with this area. They sweep for vagrants now and then, but he said we'll be fine to hide out here for a few days."

"Days?" Maria said. "I can't be gone for days."

"You'd rather be dead?"

"What about Norman? He'll file a missing person's report. What about that?"

They neared a green door. Max looked up at the huge brick building. "You said he was out of town. If we're still here by the time he gets back, we'll get word to your husband," he said, and he felt Sandra's hand grip his tight. A team again.

Playing the flashlight on the door, Sandra saw a hole that had been carved beneath the lock. She reached in and seconds later the door clicked open. "Come on," she said, waving them inside. As Max walked in, she added, "We should give PB a raise."

They all stood at the entrance and took in the massive sight — a warehouse large enough for a locomotive to pass through. An enormous empty space that reminded Max of airport hangers for jumbo jets. Sandra walked ahead, her footsteps echoing like tiny pebbles rattling on a gymnasium floor.

Plywood walls to the left formed a small office. Phallic graffiti decorated the outside. The large window pane used for a foreman to observe his workers had been shattered long ago, but a metal desk and a fan from the 1970s remained. Making a rusty screech, Sandra spun an office chair around. "Have a seat."

Max settled in, and his muscles immediately thanked him. *I might not be as unharmed as I thought.*

"Now, we wait a little," Sandra said. "The boys and Drummond should meet us here soon."

Soon turned out to be two hours. Time mostly filled with Maria sitting on the floor sobbing and Sandra assuring her that this was all temporary and that her life would return to normal fast. Max watched the woman's repeated breakdowns and build-ups and wondered what she had expected dealing with witchcraft. The history of witches was not one filled with Utopian bliss.

When the Sandwich Boys arrived, Sandra gave them each a motherly hug. Jammer J squeezed out of his, but PB simply endured. Max thought he caught PB closing his eyes and hugging back, but it only lasted an instant.

Max shook the boys' hands. "Thank you for helping us. I owe you both."

"Big time," PB said.

Sandra stood behind Max and put her hands on his shoulders. "We won't ever forget."

"I get the feeling they won't ever let us forget," Max said. "I am curious about something, though. How'd you two get back here?"

PB shrugged. "We walked."

"No, I mean how did you escape the hospital? You both were causing enough mayhem to bring in the police."

The boys shared a look. Jammer J said, "Magicians don't give up their secrets." Glancing over at Maria, he added, "She going to be okay?"

Sandra said, "This has been more than she expected. We'll get her back to her life soon, though."

Drummond floated into the office with a loud clap of his hands. "Those two boys are amazing. I got to hand it to them. They had those security guards tied up in a tizzy. I mean they never really needed my help anyway." Drummond froze as his eyes fell upon Max. "It's damn good to see you alive again."

"Thanks, partner," Max said.

PB shook his head. "You're doing it again. Talking to ghosts, right?"

With a shake he tried to hide, Jammer J said, "Man, that's screwed up. You were talkin' to the wall."

As PB and J imitated Max for each other's amusement, Max kissed Sandra's hand and said, "I think it's time for us to get working."

"You're too weak." She kissed his cheek before stepping in front of the group. "Let's all get some rest. We could use a recharge. Then we can —"

"Stop," Max said. All eyes turned onto him. "I know you're tired, and I sure know what I've been through. But getting me back was only a first step. Tucker Hull and Mother Hope have been at war with each other for decades. Maybe even longer. All that time, they've let their war simmer with small strikes against each other. But it's reached a boiling point."

"All the more reason for us to rest and be ready."

"I wish we could. This war is a big chess game. Right now, we're only a few pieces but we're important, valuable pieces — as long as we keep making moves. If we stop and rest, our enemies will have more time to study the board, and chances are, we'll become pawns again."

Maria stood. Dark mascara stained her cheeks, but her eyes were dry. "The sooner we end this, the sooner I go home, right?"

"That's right."

"Until then, I'm in danger. We all are. Right?"

"Life-threatening."

"Then I'm ready. Let's get this over with."

Sandra placed an arm around Maria, and the two women gently touched their heads together. When they looked at Max, he knew the time had come to lay out his plan. Except he didn't have one.

"Well," he said, "what have we got to deal with? Some heavy-duty curses and an underground war that's about to go public."

"And that code from Cecily Hull," Sandra said.

"Okay, then. We attack the same way we always do. We research the crap out of this until we find an angle that gives us the advantage. Except this time around, our work has to be done quietly. No personal computers, no phones, nothing traceable. We have to assume that both the Hull family and the Magi Group are using all of their resources. It's an all-out war for them. No time to hold back."

Drummond frowned. "If we've got to cut out the usual methods, how do we find Dr. Connor's corpse?"

"We don't. As long as Dr. Connor continues to be cursed, she's out of commission as far as they're all concerned. But they also know that she can become a substantial problem if caught by the other side."

Sandra nodded. "They'll keep trying to find her."

"Yup. That means dividing their forces fighting each other, looking for us, *and* looking for Dr. Connor's remains. It weakens and slows them both."

Maria said, "What if they find her?"

A look of cold confidence filled Max's eyes. "That won't happen. One thing I've learned since moving down here — these people are terrible at research. I beat them every time." He let his gaze fall on each member of the group. And then he had it — a plan. "Here's what we'll do. First, we stay in teams. Nobody goes off on their own. Sandra and Maria — you two need to research these curses. We need to know what Dr. Connor's curse is and how to break it, what happened to me, and especially, what spell or curse Mother Hope needs Dr. Connor for and how it is supposed to work against Tucker Hull."

Sandra grabbed her keys. "Is that all? You want us to discover the secret to eternal life while we're out?"

"I didn't say any of this would be easy. It's just what we've got to do."

She bent over and kissed him. "No problem. We'll come through for you."

"You already have."

She grinned and kissed him again. Max never wanted the kisses to stop.

"Okay, you two," Drummond said. "I thought we were under some pressure here."

Max chuckled. He pointed to PB and J. "You boys are to follow our enemies — particularly Mother Hope and Cecily Hull. I want to know everything they're up to. Where they go, who they talk to, everything you can. The more we know about them, the better prepared we'll be. And that all rests on you two."

The boys swelled up. "You got it, Ghostman," PB said.

"Drummond and I are going to the library."

Jammer J's eyes widened. To PB, he whispered quite loudly, "Is Drummond the ghost?"

"Yeah," PB said, putting his finger to his mouth.

Max continued, "We can't go to the library at Wake Forest. I'm a regular there and would be noticed. More importantly, Mother Hope's guard, Leon Moore, works there. So, we'll go to Thomasville."

Drummond asked, "Why Thomasville?"

"They've got a small public library. It's not a library I usually use, but they should have public access computers, so it'll be perfect to do the research I need without prying eyes upon us. I know you hate libraries, but you'll have to suck it up and deal with it this time."

"I can handle being bored. What is it we're looking into?"

"The letters Cecily Hull gave — ZSR ..." Max's brain froze.

Sandra touched Max's knees lightly. "LH. The code is ZSRLH. This all sounds good, but I think you're forgetting that I'm really better at cracking codes than you. Remember, I've done it before for us. Shouldn't I be the one working on Cecily's code?"

Max's mouth was open wide. "Not this time."

"Why not? You look strange. What is it?"

"Because it's not a code at all."

Chapter 10

BEFORE HE COULD HIT THE BOOKS, Max had to wait. First, he had to wait for the night to pass. No library was going to be open at three in the morning. Everybody found a corner of the warehouse to curl up and sleep. The nights were cool in the spring, but comfortably so. Max put his arm around Sandra and kissed the top of her head as she nuzzled his chest.

Once daylight arrived, he had to wait again. He needed a car. His was still at a body shop, and they had no way to pick it up without being noticed.

PB solved this dilemma by stealing a car — a 2012 Honda Accord. One of the most common cars in the United States. "Don't worry about driving around or passing cops or anything. I put different plates on her."

Max raised an eyebrow, and PB responded, "You didn't think I survived on the streets being a choir boy, did you?"

With Sandra and Maria off doing their research, PB and J left to follow their marks, and Max drove to the Thomasville Public Library. Drummond took the passenger seat the whole way, and Max wondered if the ghost did so just to annoy him. Especially because as compliant as Drummond was being about a trip to the library, Max knew that deep down, the ghost wanted to shout complaints the entire drive.

The library was located next to a mortuary and across from a church. Not a promising omen. Inside, the building was open and airy, particularly for such a small library.

I've been spoiled, Max thought. The library at Wake Forest University was enormous, but this one would suffice. The building had three main sections and the entrance was attached to the center section. Two islands — one at the front and one in the middle — provided the librarians with stations to do their work. The rest of the center section was composed of desks with computers or empty tables to work on. The section to the right housed the stacks. The section to the left had meeting rooms and an area devoted to children.

Max plunked down at one of the last desks with computers. He spread out his notebook, pens, and coat so that nobody else would try to share the desk. On the computer, he brought up the search tools and typed a message to Drummond: THIS WILL TAKE TIME.

"I know," Drummond said, a bit more grumpy than Max had expected.

WILL YOU KEEP AN EYE OUT FOR TROUBLE?

"Are you serious? First off, I'm always vigilant about that kind of thing. Second off, you do realize you're asking me to patrol like I'm being punished with guard duty."

THERE ARE PEOPLE TRYING TO KILL US!

"No need to get dramatic. I'm simply putting the situation in its proper perspective."

PLEASE.

"I said I would, didn't I?"

I DON'T THINK SO.

"Well, I did. Implied it, at least. So get to work already. I don't want to spend all day here, if I don't have to."

With that, Drummond floated around the room, passing though pillars and walls as well as taking a few laps around the perimeter of the building. Max cleared the search bar and typed *Z. Smith Reynolds*.

He hated that it had taken so long for him to glean the answer, but at least, he found it. After all, the Wake library was the Z. Smith Reynolds Library. ZSR. He encountered that letter combination at least once every week.

Quite quickly, he found entries that filled in the other letters — LH. Turned out to be a famous singer, Libby Holman. Reading further down, Max knew he had guessed right about the letters. Libby Holman had been married to Z. Smith. She also was accused of murdering him.

"Sounds about right for the way my cases go," Max said to the computer screen. He often talked to his research, especially when he was deep inside it, and had learned long ago not to stop. The process helped him think.

ZSRLH — Zachary Smith Reynolds and Libby Holman. Two famous people caught up in a murder. Max didn't want to jinx himself, but he couldn't help thinking that this should be easy.

He spent a short time looking into Z. Smith Reynolds. Short because there was little to find. Most of the websites spoke of him in terms of the Z. Smith Reynolds Foundation — a charity organization set up after his early and unexpected demise.

For Max, the lack of information was not surprising. His time with the Hull family had taught him how secretive the ultra-rich can be. The Reynolds family most likely thought they were controlling the information flow and protecting their name. But scandals and truths have a way of always coming to light. Eventually. That was what the Hull family never wanted to accept. They could erase all traces of family members from books and articles, but in the end, something always slipped through.

In the case of Z. Smith Reynolds, the truth came out through his wife because while Smith lived a short life, Libby Holman lived a long and thrilling life. One strange and exciting enough to garner two biographies by respected journalists and numerous entries and articles on the Internet — plus, recordings of her music on YouTube and plenty of photographs all throughout the digital world.

The more Max read, the more he became convinced that the Hulls had written ZSRLH on that file to focus on Libby. She had been living in New York City in the 1920s, doing all she could to break into show business. Singing was her main gift. She had a deep, raspy voice that seduced listeners and earned her a place on both the radio and Broadway. Her version of "Am I Blue" charted into the top ten and her song "Moanin' Low" became a huge hit. Doors opened and she stepped into a lavish, unconventional life.

Her antics behind-the-scenes became legendary. She slept with men and women like a modern-day rock star, and her beauty never seemed to fade — even after a long night of illegal drinking. Even the fact that she was Jewish did not seem to darken her star, despite it being the 1920s.

As often as the spotlight found her, however, nothing could prepare the young starlet for the attention that would turn her way when she caught the eye of Z. Smith Reynolds. The youngest of four children to RJ Reynolds, Smith struggled to find his place in life.

"Must've been hard," Max said to his research. "The older kids all made Papa proud. But not you."

Many expected for Smith to be a trust fund baby — aimless and content to live off the financial teat of the Reynolds family business. But he wasn't aimless at all. He fell in love with flying. Aviation was still new, and for a brief time, aviators grew to legendary status. Smith gained quite a bit of fame for his abilities in the cockpit. While his feats landed him in the newspapers, little of it impressed his father.

One night, while in New York City for fun, Smith stumbled into a night club and heard Libby Holman sing. She was older than him by several years, but that meant nothing to him. He was smitten.

As for Libby, she wasn't interested.

But Smith persisted, and over time, he won her love. The family, however, did not share his enthusiasm. They never embraced her — her heritage may have contributed to that — but at least she was financially independent. They could never legitimately claim that she sought the family fortune because she made more money than Smith.

Love led to marriage. Marriage to Libby, especially surrounded by a huge fortune, led to wild parties and embarrassing newspaper articles. Yet despite their cavalier behavior while most suffered through the Great Depression, the public loved the couple.

"Until it all changed," Max said.

It happened after the July 4th party of 1932. Reynolda House — the large Reynolds estate that bordered Wake Forest University — had been the scene of a raucous evening. Smith and Libby had a gaggle of friends over to drink and celebrate. Alcohol flowed, people danced, and many found excuses to walk off together into the woods.

But during the party, Smith acted rather morose. He showed little interest in the festivities and spent much of the time avoiding most of the people. For a while, he wandered about searching for Libby. Nobody knew where she had gone.

Staying at the house with Smith and Libby were Albert Walker, Smith's childhood friend who worked for him as a personal assistant, and also Blanche Yurka, a lovely actress from New York City. Finally, there was W. E. Fulcher, the groundskeeper and sometimes night watchmen. That night, after the revelers had all left and the houseguests had gone to sleep, Fulcher walked around the building and saw the shameful way the house had been left.

Empty bottles of alcohol, trash, food, broken glasses — one could easily mistake the scene for the remnants of an end-of-the-year frat party. Libby and Smith seemed to think somebody else would come along and clean it all up. Fulcher knew they were right. As he roamed the property, he heard the gunshot snap, and the world slipped from under him.

Libby and Albert came thumping downstairs, crying out that Z. Smith Reynolds had shot himself. Along with Ms. Yurka, they carried Smith outside and placed him in the back of a car. Careening through the streets, Albert drove to the hospital as fast as possible for a car in 1932.

With everyone covered in blood and acting hysterical, the hospital staff had a hard time piecing together what had happened. Over the hours, however, the story developed that Smith was drunk and angry. He argued with Libby, claiming she had taken up an affair with Albert — he swore they went into the woods together — and he would not live like a cuckolded fool. Libby tried to reason with him, but Smith put the gun to his head and fired.

"Except it won't be so cut and dry," Max said as he wrote down the main points of the story.

Indeed, the tale Libby presented began falling apart quite rapidly. At the hospital, Albert had stated that he heard a gunshot and came running into the porch bedroom; however, Libby said that she met Albert in the hallway. Ms. Yurka seemed to agree with both accounts.

Things became stranger when the oddly named Sheriff Transou Scott attempted to investigate the crime scene. All inquiries into the shooting met stiff resistance from Reynolda company men. When Sheriff Scott asked to see Libby or Ms. Yurka for questioning, he was told they had both been heavily sedated and were unable to come downstairs.

This caused Scott to push harder. He wanted to search the porch bedroom for the murder weapon. The Reynolda men refused to let him up. Eventually, they had no choice since their lawyers could only obstruct for so long. Yet when Sheriff Scott finally made it upstairs to the bedroom, it had been cleaned up.

Three times, the room was searched for the gun allegedly used by Z. Smith. Three times, they came up empty. Later, however, the Reynolda men convinced Scott to look once more. This fourth time, the gun was found sitting in plain sight.

Max wrote furiously, his hands trying to keep up with the thoughts in his head. Clearly, the Reynolda men covered up whatever had happened, but Max suspected they didn't know themselves. They only knew that the boss's son was dead and the wife was in a bad position — all of which had to be kept as quiet as possible. Of course, they knew this would hit the papers, but ideally, it would be a sensational story for a few days that would then wrap up as a tragic suicide. Even back then, some people understood the importance of controlling the narrative.

Except that pain-in-the-ass Sheriff Scott refused to accept their version of events. One of the big problems was that, even in 1932, the medical examiner was able to determine that the gun had not been pressed against Smith's temple as described for his suicide. Instead, the weapon had been held at a distance and angle which suggested someone else had pulled the trigger.

Adding to the circus, the coroner, Mr. Dalton, held a secret inquest at Reynolda House in which all the "evidence" was presented. A judge and all the requisite authorities were invited and partook in the proceedings — all except Sheriff Scott. When Scott learned of this, he blew up. But the excuse given was that only in this way could they respectfully handle the case without turning the Reynolds family into a gawker's paradise.

In the end, the inquest determined that Z. Smith Reynolds did not commit suicide but rather classified his death as a homicide. Thus, the inquest had the opposite result of what the Reynolda men had hoped. Perhaps. Because while a homicide kept the family tragedy hot in the news, it also pointed the finger directly at Libby Holman.

Max suspected the situation was more complex and less nefarious. Reynolds was both a family and a massive company. With so many people and so many jobs that could be made or destroyed by shifts of power in the family, there were plenty of competing angles. More than any single person probably knew.

While Libby was brought into court, the charges never stuck. All the evidence available could barely be called circumstantial, and all the evidence that could have been useful had been swept away under the careful control of the company men.

As strange and harrowing as that entire experience had been for Libby, things did not calm in the years after. Her life would continue to be filled with odd tragedies. Max scribbled faster — noting dates and key events. The picture of her Shakespearian history formed in his head as he wrote.

Drummond interrupted his work with a single, terrible word. "Trouble."

A police officer had entered the library. He had a muscular, fit look with buzzed hair and slim sunglasses worn backwards as if he had eyes on the back of his head. Leaning on the checkout counter, he spoke confidentially to a librarian — a mousy gal who seemed troubled by what the officer had said. Both of them paused to scan the library.

Max ducked his head behind the computer monitor on the desk. "How could cops have found me already?"

"They didn't," Drummond said. "Not you specifically. But maybe this guy stumbled on your stolen car."

"Great. Now what?"

"Don't get frazzled. You've been in jams before. You can handle this."

"Easy for you. You can pass through a wall. If they jail me, I'm not going anywhere."

The librarian walked into an enclosed section while the cop continued to search the floor with his eyes. Drummond said, "At least, this guy's not moving. That suggests he's not looking for you directly. But he might be trying to find anybody acting suspicious."

"You mean like a guy hiding behind a computer talking to an invisible ghost?"

"Yeah, like that."

Max closed his notebook. He could not get back to work — too risky if they were wrong and the police officer was targeting him — but he could not stay hidden behind a computer monitor either. He tucked the notebook under his arm and walked amongst the stacks.

Using the tall shelves of endless books as cover, he worked his way toward the front of the library. He would not be able to get out this way — the stacks were on the opposite side of the exit. If he tried to leave through the entranceway, he would have to walk right by the officer. However, he could remain hidden by the books and observe.

Buying time is better than being a sitting duck.

The librarian returned, leaned far over the counter, and whispered something to the cop. As she pulled back, Max swore he saw a devilish smile on her face. Then she walked away. She went to the far side of the floor and through a door that appeared to lead to offices. Less than thirty seconds later, the cop followed the same path.

Drummond snickered. "Looks like the cop's here for something other than you."

"Let's go. We don't know how long they'll be."

"Good thinking. He might be a quick performer."

Max's stomach clenched as he stepped away from the cover of the stacks. He walked around the checkout island and toward the exit, giving a nod and smile to another librarian. As he pushed the exit door open, Drummond turned back.

"You go ahead," he said. "I'll delay the cop if he gets done early or is called on duty or something."

Max wanted to stop and yell at the ghost. They were partners, a team, and Drummond was going to ditch him for a peepshow. But he knew if he said any of that, the cop would have come out to see the disturbance, and if he was lucky, Max would only be carted off to a mental institution for observation. If he was unlucky, the cop worked for Hull or Mother Hope.

Picking up the pace, Max hurried around the corner to the parking lot. He continually peered over his shoulder, half-expecting the cop to come sprinting out with his pants unbuckled and his shirt askew. But the cop never arrived. Instead, when Max looked toward his car, he discovered the real threat — a man in a suit and tie leaning against the car, his arms folded across his chest and a toothpick in his mouth.

"Max," the man said as if they were old chums. "I'd like to borrow that notebook of yours."

Chapter 11

MAX CLUTCHED THE NOTEBOOK against his side. He could try to run, but he did not trust his legs. Though his strength had returned quickly from being immobile for so long, his muscles still complained. Adrenaline would provide some needed boost, but it wouldn't last long enough — not against a guy like this. He was young and fit. No, running was not an option.

"Who sent you?" he asked, not moving closer to the car nor heading back to the library.

The man opened his hands. "Does it really matter?"

"Actually, it does. There are a lot of players in this thing. You should know what side you're on."

"I don't take sides. I'm freelance. Wherever the money is, that's the side I'm on."

"Any chance you can be bought off to change sides?"

The man tapped his forehead. "Not too smart. If I do that, word gets out and I lose all my business. Might even lose my life, depending on who I cross."

Sweat dampened Max's arms. His only way out was for the cop to finish up so that Drummond would float outside, but Max Porter's unlucky star shined brightly above him — looked like the cop would be taking his sweet time. "My notes won't help anybody else. It's not like I wrote down some big secret and underlined it."

"Not my problem. I was told to get your notebook. That's what I'm going to do. Now, I can see that you're an intelligent man and that you already understand this situation quite clearly. So, if you simply hand over the notebook, I'll leave. Won't even have to touch you."

"You're not going to kill me?"

The man laughed. "Not for what they're paying."

"What if we struck a bargain?"

The man pushed off the car and strolled over. Max inched back a few steps. When the man reached out and touched the notebook, a volcano of rage erupted within Max.

He shoved the man hard. The surprise move tripped the man and he fell on the pavement. Max leaped over and raced to his car. His fingers fumbled for his keys.

"Shouldn't have done that," the man said.

As Max found the right key, the man clamped down on Max's hand. He twisted the hand, and the keys hit the ground with a jangle. Three fast punches followed — two to the gut, doubling Max over, and one to the back of the head.

The man grabbed hold of the notebook, but Max refused to let go. For a second, they locked in a tug-of-war. But then the man kicked Max in the side. The air whooshed out of Max's lungs and he tumbled over. Cradling his stomach and his side, he rocked on the ground, desperate for enough air to stand but knowing it was too late.

By the time he could breathe, the man was gone and so was the notebook.

Max drove back to the empty tobacco warehouse and curled on the desk. He had several hours to wait until the others arrived. All through the drive back, he thought of what he would say to Drummond, but now that he had time to cool off, he decided to say nothing directly. He knew the ghost too well. Once Drummond learned what had happened and what they had lost, the old ghost would beat himself up plenty. A more productive use of Max's time was to go over the Libby Holman story as much as possible, to keep it fresh in his head.

When evening arrived and the team converged on Max, he told them everything about Libby. From her early days to her marriage to the murder, he left nothing out. Then, he had to admit to losing his notebook. Sandra jumped to his side and lifted his shirt to inspect his bruises.

Drummond's face dropped all sense of warmth. "I'm sorry, Max. I should have been there."

"You're damn right," Sandra said. "We're all in danger. What were you thinking leaving Max alone? Especially when he's still recovering."

Max pushed down his shirt. "It's okay. I'm okay. There was a cop in the library. Drummond was making sure I got into my stolen car without getting noticed." Though Drummond gave Max a thankful nod, he clearly agreed with Sandra — he had failed his partner. Before Sandra could weigh in on the excuse given, Max went on, "There's more to the Libby Holman story."

"More?" Drummond perked up.

"I wish I had my notes. I wrote it down as fast as I could, figuring I'd be able to check it all later. Guess that plan didn't work out, did it? Still, even if I get the details wrong, the basic idea is right."

PB and J had been listening like two kids in the 1930s sitting next to the family radio. Living on the streets had taught them a lot — including life without television or the Internet. They wiggled in their seats, eager for more story. Even Maria inched closer to hear the rest.

"They never could pin anything on Libby, but she wasn't truly free either. One of the big problems through the whole thing was that Libby was pregnant. She and Smith supposedly had been trying to have a child but he was unable. Some speculation came about that she was pregnant with Albert's child, that Smith found out, which led to an altercation resulting in his death. That may have been true, but nobody could prove if that death was intentional or accidental. Nobody could prove anything."

Max leaned forward as the story unfolded in his mind. The Reynolds family fought a little regarding the will, but not much. The death of Smith was enough of a blow. They didn't want any more publicity of that kind. Libby was gracious. She accepted a payout and the bulk of the estate went to a trust for her son, Christopher.

"Several years later," Max said, "she married an actor named Holmes. This was 1939, I think. She met the guy after dating his older brother. The next year, both brothers joined the Canadian Air Force and the older one died in a collision. I don't think it was a battle — this was during World War II — but perhaps a training exercise. I didn't have time to look into those details.

"Anyway, Libby's husband comes home at the end of the war, and like many couples dealing with being apart for so many years, they found they no longer knew each other. They separated and before the year was out, Holmes overdosed on barbiturates."

Maria covered her mouth. "She lost two husbands? That's horrible."

"It gets worse. Five years later, in 1950, her son wanted to go mountain climbing with a buddy. She gave her permission, and the two headed up Mount Whitney, the highest peak in California. Neither boy knew enough to attempt such a climb, and they paid for it with their lives. This devastated Libby. She never forgave herself.

"Over the years to come, she buried her grief in work. Got involved in the Civil Rights movement and became close friends with Martin Luther King and his wife, Coretta. She helped finance the defense of the famous pediatrician, Dr. Spock, after he was arrested for antiwar demonstrations.

"She even married a third time — Louis something — Shecker, Shaker — no, it was Schanker. Louis Schanker. They married in 1960 or so. But as the 60s went on, she suffered severe depression. The deaths of the Kennedys, of Martin Luther King, the Vietnam War, her own son's death, and in 1966, the loss of her one-time lover Montgomery Clift — it all was too much for her. She tried to commit suicide several times. In June 1971, she succeeded. Used her Rolls Royce and a closed garage."

Max took a few deep breaths. He felt like he had been running a sprint. "That's it. That's all I can remember."

"That's a lot," Sandra said.

"Except it doesn't mean anything. She had a wild, tragic life that touched one of the Winston-Salem big families, and that's it. I didn't find any connection to the Hulls or to the Magi Group."

"If there's a connection to be found, we'll find it."

"Maybe. If I had my notes to look over, I'm sure I'd find something in there. All the details are on those pages."

Drummond said, "That's why they stole the notebook."

"Except they won't get anything out of it. We've gone up against Hull's researchers before. They're not smart enough to find the needle in the haystack of my notes."

"So, why worry about it?" Sandra asked. "You gave us a lot of information to work with."

"I just have the gnawing feeling that if I had more time with my notes, I'd see it — whatever *it* is."

"Um," Maria said, "why don't you go to another library? Finish your research there?"

"I might have to. But they found me this time which means they're following me."

Sandra gestured to the Sandwich Boys. "We all have things to report. Maybe something we say will line up the dots for you and save you the trouble. What did you two find?"

PB lifted his chin and made sure all were paying attention before he spoke. "Well, let me tell you. The whole thing was very strange. I stole a red hatchback so that I could follow Mother Hope wherever she went. I started with that Leon guy at the University. I figured Mother Hope would be pissed off about Max getting out of the hospital, and I was right. She showed up and talked outside with Leon. She spoke real worried-like. She had big muscle with her, too. He drove their car. I followed them all the way to Greensboro — went right by two speed traps and the cops didn't even look at me."

"Let me guess," Max said. "She went to the O. Henry Hotel."

"That's right. Holed up there and never came out."

"That's home plate for the Magi Group. What about you,

Jammer? How did it go following Cecily Hull around?"

Jammer J straightened into a decent impression of PB. "She went downtown and stopped at a few apartment buildings. She'd be in there for maybe twenty minutes or so and then go on to the next one. Then she drove out of town. But I only got a bike. Worked fine following her around city streets, but once she got on Business 40, I couldn't follow her."

"That's okay. You did what you could."

"I did better than that. I ain't some fool who just gives up. I figured if I couldn't follow her, I could follow what she'd already done. I went back and checked those buildings. There were four apartments she visited. Two were unmarked, but two of them were businesses. You'll love this. They were both fortune tellers."

PB gave J a high-five. "Great job! What's that mean? She's nuts?"

Max said, "I don't know what it means. But if you think going to a fortune teller makes her crazy, you must think I should be committed. I talk to ghosts."

"Only one ghost."

With a soft chuckle, Sandra said, "Don't dismiss her even if we find out she is crazy. Sane or not, she's dangerous."

Max shifted to face his wife. "How did you do? Find anything about the curses?"

Sandra pointed to Maria. Maria stood like a schoolgirl from the 1950s about to give a report. "We didn't find much, but then I didn't expect us to. These curses are old. Ancient, really. And everything we could turn up pointed to texts that I don't have."

Jolting at her words, Max said, "You went to your house?"

"Where were we supposed to go? The library doesn't carry these kinds of books. Besides, I had to call my husband. It was one thing for me to be out for a night. But if he didn't hear from me soon, he'd know something was wrong."

"You didn't tell him where we are, did you?"

"I'm not an idiot."

Max looked at Sandra. "You let her do this?"

Sandra smacked Max's chest with the back of her hand. "Don't you dare start that again. I made a judgment call, and if you'd shut up and listen to her, you'd find out what we did learn."

Perhaps sensing that she should step in before a marital spat ignited further, Maria said, "These books aren't the normal ones on curses. Only a few witches, really old witches or those in old families, would have them. If anybody in North Carolina qualifies, it is Madame Vansandt. She's been my mentor ever since I became a witch. She taught me everything I know."

"And she'll help us?" Max asked, his tone dropping back.

"Hopefully. She's ninety-seven, so she can be a bit ornery."

Drummond said, "There's also the problem that she's a witch. Contacting this old broad means contacting the world of witches in a much more serious way than we have already with this case. That's not going to be good for us. I don't like it."

Max agreed. "Anybody got other suggestions?"

Nobody said a word.

"That kind of settles it, then. Most important thing is that we've got to keep making moves. Even if they aren't the best ones — because with the forces we're up against, anything is a better move than standing still. Dealing with witches can get tricky, but right now, that's all we've got." He looked over his team. Despite being tired and stressed, they all appeared eager. "Okay. Let's go see the witch."

Chapter 12

AFTER A NIGHT WITH LITTLE REST, the group's collective stomachs growled. Nobody had eaten in over twenty-four hours. Neither had they bathed.

"I'll get the food," Jammer J said.

As he walked out, PB stretched his arms behind his head. "Don't worry. He's really good at getting food without getting caught."

"There's a bathroom in our office," Sandra said. "It's only a few blocks from here. Maybe we should risk it."

Max sniffed his armpit. "We are rather ripe. But we can't go to the office. They found me all the way out in Thomasville. They definitely have our office staked out."

"Then what?"

Like a king satisfied with his own brain, he said, "We've got a couple cars. Let's drive out on Route 40, west toward the mountains. We can use one of those stops that cater truckers. They have showers, and if we're careful — take different routes, take multiple detours — we can make sure nobody follows us."

Twenty minutes later, Jammer J returned with five bananas and a loaf of bread. Everybody downed a banana sandwich — PB ate two — before loading up in the cars and heading out of town. They couldn't do much about their clothes, but at least they wouldn't be visiting Madame Vansandt smelling like refuse.

By noon, they were back in Winston-Salem. Max sent the Sandwich Boys off to trail Mother Hope and Cecily Hull while the rest of the team visited Madame Vansandt. The old witch lived in an apartment building several blocks north of the baseball stadium on a revitalized section of Broad Street.

As they parked in a small off-street lot, Maria said, "She used to live further up, but her old place got condemned and then they built these apartments a few years ago."

Maria had a new bounce in her walk. She confessed that she had not been Madame Vansandt's pupil for several years and was both excited and nervous to see the witch once again.

Drummond did not share her enthusiasm. "Nobody should be that happy to see a witch."

Sandra scowled at him but said nothing.

They climbed a stairwell to the third floor of the seven-story building. A sign with the word OPEN hung from the apartment door. Maria walked straight inside, never breaking her gait. The others followed.

The apartment proved to be every bit of a witch's home. Filled with dusty volumes and dim lights, the furnishings made the new building seem old and small. Heavy tapestries hung on the walls next to astrological charts and a poster of the human nervous system with acupuncture points marked. At least, Max hoped they were acupuncture points. On a small table with fringe cloth hanging over the edges, Max noticed a tiny bell and a stack of business cards.

MADAME VANSANDT
SPELLS, POTIONS, AND MORE
MEDIUM SERVICES AVAILABLE UPON REQUEST

"My oh my," a creaking voice with a thick North Carolina accent said. From a hall in the back, Madame Vansandt appeared. She was taller than Max had imagined and had long, bony fingers that wrapped lightly around the handles of her walker. Though the room was dark, she wore sunglasses that formed a black block across her eyes and shaded the sides as well. Her vibrant smile glinted with life as she inspected each new face. Though heavily wrinkled, her skin clung to a dignified beauty that must have been stunning in her prime.

"Madame," Maria said as she rushed over to embrace her mentor.

"Maria Cortez-Kane. I am delighted to see you. Truly, I am. It warms my heart to know that we can talk one last time."

"What do you mean *one last time?*"

Madame Vansandt brushed her fingers along Maria's cheek. "Child, my brain works fine. I know how old I am. Every morning I wake up is a blessing. Every night I close my eyes, I wonder if I will have the pleasure of opening them again."

"Don't talk like that."

"Why not? It's the truth." She wheeled her walker over to a plush, high-backed chair. "Be a dear, and help me sit down."

As Maria rushed over, Drummond read the titles of the books on one shelf. "I'm starting to like this gal. She's still got spunk. I never got to live that long, but I always thought I'd either end up a bitter, old fool or I'd be like her."

Sandra walked closer to Madame Vansandt. "Maria suggested we come here to meet you."

"Oh?" Madame Vansandt said. "What do you want with an old crow like me?"

"We need some advice about a few curses."

"Nasty business. I don't deal with that kind of thing anymore."

Drummond clicked his tongue. "For a witch that doesn't deal with that stuff, she's sure got a lot of books on the subject."

"Please," Max said. "We only need you to answer a few questions."

Maria clasped Madame Vansandt's hand between hers. "Things have changed out beyond your doors. It's not like it was. There's a war brewing."

"Bless your heart." The old witch patted Maria's hands. "You really think I don't know what happens in my backyard? The war, dear child, has gone on for a long time. Well over a century. Not always with the same players or the same pieces, but I assure you, this is nothing new. You are right about one thing, though. There is something brewing. But it is the end, not the beginning, that sits on our horizon."

Maria bowed her head and kissed Madame Vansandt's knuckles. "These people here, they're all caught up in this mess, and they've dragged me into it, too. If you can help them with their curse, then I can be done with them and get back to my life."

Madame Vansandt pulled her fingers free. "That won't happen."

"Please."

"You misunderstand, but then you always did. Always jumping ahead of me before I finished a sentence."

"I'm not trying to jump ahead. It's just that my life's been hijacked, and —"

Covering Maria's mouth and jaw with her whole hand, Madame Vansandt said, "Shh. Begging won't change the fact that there is no returning to your old life. Once you set onto the road of being a witch, once you've pulled back the gauze and exposed your open heart to the real world of magic, once you had cast your first spell, your former life disappeared. Vanished into the ether. What you think you had was merely you playing house. The real world has finally caught you, as it does with all witches. There is no going back." She turned her head towards Sandra. "Even for the amateur."

Sandra's nostrils flared. "I'm more than an amateur, more than some wannabe poking around the edges. Your pupil and I broke a curse and brought my husband back from near death."

"Let me see this husband." Waving her arms like a grandmother seeking a hug, Madame Vansandt ushered Max over. She looked him up and down, kneaded his arms and shoulders, and then gestured for him to turn in a circle. Finally, she settled back in her chair. "Like I said — amateur. I am truly sorry to tell you this, sir, but you are still cursed."

"What?" Max said.

"Oh, for novices, your wife and my Maria did a remarkable job restoring you to your body, that much is evident, but they failed to break the curse through and through. If you don't believe me, look at your chest in the mirror."

Max ignored his sudden queasiness and stood in front of a narrow mirror hanging on one wall. He pulled on the collar of his shirt until he saw it — the edges of the curse marked on his body.

Sandra's quizzical yet worried face peeked over his shoulder. "I'm so sorry."

"Don't be. You brought me back."

Stepping away from the mirror, he tried to remain calm as he faced Madame Vansandt. "So, what does this mean for me?"

"Only that you're not free of your situation. Yes, you are back in your body, but you are not anchored to it. With a little effort and some magical know-how, whoever did this to you could send your body back into whatever state it was — probably a coma — and return you to the world of ghosts."

Maria pulled away from her mentor. "Then what do we do? How do I get back?"

"Oh for crying out loud." Sandra whirled on Maria. "Don't you listen? You chose to be a witch and that's that. You wanted to know the secrets. You wanted to gain the power. Well, you got it. You don't get to stir a hornet's nest and then complain that you got stung."

Flinching at the verbal assault, Maria backed toward the corner of the room. Max could hear the woman stifling her tears. Though he understood why his wife had lashed out, he figured it would be best to bring things back into focus. After all, no good could come from causing such a scene in front of an old witch.

Crouching before Madame Vansandt, Max said, "My wife and I have dealt with many types of spells before. We can handle a lot more than most give us credit for. And, frankly, we don't have a choice. Either we break this curse or we suffer under it."

"I never said you couldn't break the curse."

Sandra came back. "How? What do I have to do?"

"You? What can a beginner like you do? Oh, I grant that you pulled off a complicated spell for your husband, but this curse — this isn't stirring a hornet's nest. This is a bear cave with twenty hibernating beasts waiting to rip you to pieces."

"I can handle it."

"Really, now? So bold and proud. But this is high-level magic. This is the kind of thing that requires serious sacrifice. Years of hard work and strict discipline."

"You don't seem to understand. The man cursed here is my husband. I love my husband. Even if it takes the rest of my life, I'll put in the time. I'll do whatever is necessary to break that curse."

From behind her thick shades, Madame Vansandt's eyebrows rose. "I see. This is about love, is it? Then come here. Come close."

Though a slight tremor flickered along Sandra's fingers, she stepped forward. Max tried to get her attention, tried to shake his head subtly, but she either failed to get the message or simply ignored him.

Drummond swished in front of her. "Don't go near her. Something's not right about her. And I don't mean because she's a witch."

A hard look from Sandra forced Drummond to step aside. Two more strides and she stood directly in front of the witch. She lowered her head until they were close enough to kiss.

Madame Vansandt's lips broke into a wide grin. "Oh, you are bold. You think you're capable of sacrifice, do you? You think you're capable of committing a real sacrifice. Perhaps even your eye?" She whipped off her shades. A dark, grisly hole gaped at Sandra. The old woman cackled as Sandra recoiled. Maria broke down to the floor gasping and crying.

"I told you," Drummond said. "Damn witches. There's always a cost with them. She probably wants revenge on whoever took her eye out."

Pointing to where her right eye should have been, Madame Vansandt said, "You want to break your lover's curse? I want my eye back. Get me my eye and I'll give you what you want."

"Even worse than I thought."

Before Sandra could protest, Madame Vansandt lifted her head and pointed to a bookshelf. "Get the one marked with three pentagrams."

Drummond indicated the book. "Be careful. Listen to me this time."

Sandra selected the book, raised an eyebrow at Drummond, and returned to the witch. "Here."

"Thank you." Madame Vansandt put her shades back on. "Now, I am not trying to insult you or your abilities. But we all have limits, dear, and at the moment, yours are that of a novice. You will need a strong witch to break this curse. A strong witch for a strong spell, and a location of great negative energy to cast it." She thumbed through the book until she found the desired page. "There. You find a capable witch and the right place to do it in. You get me my eye, and then I'll use this spell to —"

Three strong knocks pounded on the door.

Max looked over, then to the witch. The book was gone. He wanted to check under her chair or beneath the side table, but the pounding continued.

"Come in already. The sign says *Open*," Madame Vansandt said in a crass tone that did not suit her.

"Wait," Max said not turning away from the witch. "Where do we get your eye?"

She grinned without joy. "That would be with a Hull."

The door opened and PB bustled in. "They're coming. You've got to get out of here."

"Who's coming?" Sandra asked.

"Everyone. Hulls, Magi — their war's firing up and they're coming on down here for the battle."

Chapter 13

"CALM DOWN, KID." Max closed the front door. "Tell us what's happened."

PB gave a sideways glance at Madame Vansandt before moving closer to Sandra. "I did as you asked me. I followed Mother Hope again, and just like before she went into the O. Henry Hotel and didn't come out. I got bored, and I figured if she won't come out, I could sneak in and spy on her."

"You shouldn't have done that. It's too dangerous."

"Why? A couple of uptight people at the counter and two bodyguards so pumped full of steroids they probably have no balls. Besides, I'm here, ain't I?"

"I just meant —"

"No time for this crap. Listen. I got in, hid under a room service cart, and ended up in her office. Sat there for two hours before she said anything worth hearing. Leon Moore called — she had him on speaker — and I heard him saying they followed you here to this witch's place. Then he said that one of his spies called him saying that Tucker Hull had sent a hit squad over here. Mother Hope yelled at him saying he had to grab you right away. I slipped out, got in my car, and raced over here."

A sour taste filled Max's mouth. He swallowed hard against it. "They're all coming here?"

"That's what I been saying. We've got to go."

"Hold on. You were in Greensboro. That's a forty minute drive. How did you beat them? Shouldn't Leon have taken us by now?"

"Mother Hope told him to get a ward before coming here.

Protection against ghosts and witches. She talked a bunch of crazy stuff like that — I figure, when you get a lucky break, you take it and don't ask questions."

Sandra had moved to the balcony window. "Looks like Leon's finally arrived."

Tapping on his leg, Max observed Madame Vansandt. "Tucker's men probably had to get wards, too. They're really scared of you."

"Hey," Drummond said. "Wards could be for me. You know I can be plenty scary."

Max checked out the window. Leon had three men with him, all dressed in gray suits and carrying handguns like classic G-men from a 1950s movie. Only thing missing were the hats.

As Leon pointed out positions for his men to take, Max heard Madame Vansandt snapping her fingers. He glanced back. She glared at Maria until the woman rose from her cowering corner and walked over with head bowed.

"Be a kind dear and fetch me a red candle."

To Max's astonishment, Maria gave a quick curtsy before heading into an adjacent room. After she left, the old witch opened a drawer on the side table and picked up a pen and pad. She bent over the pad and wrote.

Drummond flew in through the wall. Max jumped — he had not realized the ghost had left. "I was right," Drummond said. "Those wards bounce me off like a pinball hit by lightning. I can't get close to any of the Magi people."

Max went to the front door, stopped, and came back. "We've got to leave here."

Following Max back and forth, PB said, "That's what I'm telling you."

"We can't go walk out the lobby door, though." His mind rushed through his limited options. He pointed to Sandra. "I need you to take everyone up to the roof."

"The roof?" Sandra said as her jaw set in defiance.

"Down's not an option, so up seems the only direction."

"Until there's no more up to go."

"I didn't say the idea had no flaws, but it's the only one

we've got."

"Then, here's an idea for you. I'm staying to fight by your side." Before Max could step close to her, lower his voice, and attempt to persuade her, Sandra put out her hand. "Don't even try. We're a team, so I'm not going anywhere."

"Honey, I —"

But Maria entered directly between them as she brought a wide-based, red candle over to Madame Vansandt. She placed it on the floor and looked up like a puppy expecting a pat on the head. Instead, the old witch handed her the pad. "Now, get these ingredients and grind them in a bowl. You remember where I keep everything?"

"Yes, ma'am."

"Good girl. Hop to it."

Sandra stepped next to Max and whispered. "I've already lost you once. That was enough."

He clasped her hand.

PB had moved to the window. "Tucker's men are here. At least, I think it's them." Two gunshots pinged off a car's roof. "Yup, it's them."

Gunfire erupted below in a constant barrage like a hailstorm smacking into the ground. Max and Sandra joined PB and peeked over the lip of the windowsill. One suited man dashed between two cars in the parking lot. A bullet caught him in the leg. With a hand staunching the blood, he limped toward a red Prius. Another bullet clocked his head back and sprayed blood next to the car.

"Don't watch," Sandra said to PB.

PB snorted a laugh. "You don't think I ever seen somebody shot before?"

From the ceiling, Drummond said, "Don't worry about him. The kid's tough."

Max didn't think PB looked all that tough. He talked tough, but his face had lost a lot of color, and he flinched with each gunshot.

Maria entered the room again with a small bowl of grainy, brown powder. She set it next to the candle. Madame Vansandt handed her a piece of chalk and watched Maria draw a circle around the chair.

Max pushed away from the window and back to Madam Vansandt. The powder smelled of rotting fruit. "Whatever your spell is, I sure hope you can pull it off fast."

"This is for me. You're on your own." To Maria, she added, "Light the candle and hand me the bowl."

"Leon's men are falling back," Sandra said. "They're coming inside."

As if responding to her words, gunshots could be heard beneath them along with glass breaking and several residents crying or shouting. Max paced between the front door and the window.

Think, think. They had no chance of getting downstairs. That was obvious. And they had no real weapons. Max owned a handgun, but he kept it locked in his office desk. He hadn't been there since going to the party that ended in the hospital.

He glanced at Madame Vansandt. She held her head over the bowl as though she had a cold and cleared her sinuses with steaming water. Her mouth moved but made no sound. No help there.

More gunfire. An anguished grunt.

"I don't mean to nag," Drummond said, "but you ain't got much time left."

Max's mouth gaped open. "Gee, you think?" Taking Sandra's hand, he said, "Okay, we're all getting out of here. Let's move to a different floor. We've got to buy some time. Hold out until —"

Sirens screeched outside.

"— the police arrive. Okay, then. Help is here. Come on, everyone. One floor up and we'll just have to wait."

Max, Sandra, and PB gathered by the front door. Sandra reached out toward Maria, but Maria shook her head. "I'm staying," she said and sat at Madame Vansandt's feet.

"Drummond, go check the hall for us," Max said.

Drummond swooped in, stuck his head through the wall, and popped back. "All clear."

"Here we go." Max opened the door. He stepped out and looked to the right. The Pale Man entered the hall from the stairwell. They held each other's gaze. Then the Pale Man lifted his gun and grinned, flashing his silver incisor.

Leaping backward, Max plowed into the rest of the team, toppling them back into the room. Two gunshots splintered the door jamb. Two more shots fired off from the other end of the hall.

"You okay, Max?" Leon Moore called out.

With his foot, Max kicked the door shut before standing up. He whipped around to face Drummond. "You call that *clear?*"

"Hey, it was clear when I looked."

Max rushed across the room to the sofa. "PB. Help." Together, the two moved the sofa perpendicular to the wall. Sandra hurried over. It wasn't going to protect them at all — a bullet would have no trouble ripping through it — but it made them feel better.

Outside, a voice on a megaphone said, "Stop firing and come out, hands up!"

PB rushed over to the window. "Is that all they're gonna do?"

"Get back here," Sandra said, scurrying after him. Max reached out, but his fingers slipped on the back of Sandra's blouse.

The front door smashed open. With guns firing, the Pale Man and another entered. Three shots, spread across the room to suppress any brave soul. Sandra and Max flattened on the ground. Despite PB's rough experiences, he spun in surprise to face the gunfire. Max waved his hand for the boy to drop, but PB only looked at the guns.

The Pale Man stepped in, his grim, clenched jaw grinding away as he saw Madame Vansandt sitting in her chair. He cocked his head at PB and though he returned his sly gaze at the witch, he had no trouble firing at his new target. PB's shoulder wrenched back as his face slackened.

And Madame Vansandt's spell went off.

A bright rosy light snapped out of the circle along with a

deafening and brief noise. For a moment, Max couldn't see and his ears buzzed with a high-pitched note. *A flash-bang? She made a flash-bang?*

But as his sight returned, he saw the spell had been more than that. A yellow light plumed across the room like smoke from a bomb. Time slowed around them. Max had no idea if that was the result of adrenaline pumping through his body or if the spell had actually slowed time. Either way, he knew he had to move.

Everyone had fallen to the floor, clasping hands over ears or rubbing their eyes. All except Madame Vansandt. As Max shoved off the floor, feeling like he moved underwater, he saw her rise into the air. A sphere of golden light surrounded her like a painting of an Old Testament prophet and she floated gently forward.

No time to follow her. Max figured if he could find the strength to get up, the others would, too. He stumbled to Sandra and helped her to her feet. Once up, she went to PB. Max turned to the Pale Man and his accomplice. Thankfully, both had taken Madame Vansandt's spell head on.

The accomplice had been knocked out cold. But the Pale Man had managed to get to his knees. Madame Vansandt floated by his head and he lifted a weak arm to stop her. She ignored him and drifted through the open front door.

Max followed right up behind and kicked the Pale Man in the side of the head. Not sporting at all, but when dealing with contract killers, Max figured sporting wasn't too important. As his foot made contact, as Madame Vansandt left the room, time returned to normal. The Pale Man dropped down. Dazed or unconscious, Max didn't know, and he had no intention of taking a chance at finding out.

"We've got to get out of here now," he said, "before the cops come up."

Sandra frowned and pointed to her ear.

Speaking slower and louder, Max said, "We've got to go. Cops coming."

Sandra took hold of PB by the right arm — blood stained

his left shoulder — while Maria still sat on the floor by Madame Vansandt's empty chair. Max pointed to the front door. "Take PB up to the roof. I'll get her."

He squatted before her and gently lifted her chin with two fingers.

A tear spilled from Maria's eye. "She left me here. I was a good pupil. I did everything she ever asked of me. And she left me here."

Though her words were muddled by his ringing ears, he understood enough. "You can't trust a witch."

"But I'm a witch. And your wife is, too."

"I don't know what to call the two of you, but you're not witches. Not like that."

Maria looked straight into Max. "How can you be sure?"

He smiled back. "Because you didn't leave us." He stood and opened his hand. "Come on. We'll get through this. We always do. But we do it together."

Like a shell-shocked soldier, she accepted his help standing and left the apartment with him. Her hands were cold and clammy, but Max did not let go. He guided her down the bullet-riddled hall, to the stairwell, and up to the roof.

With any luck, and that was a questionable qualification, Max hoped they could recoup up there while the police spent a few hours sifting through this mess. They would probably canvas the neighbors and a few businesses up and down the street, but he saw little reason they would check the roof. Any way he looked at it, though, they were going be stuck for a long time — and PB was losing blood fast.

Chapter 14

CLIMBING THE STAIRS TOOK LONGER than Max had expected. With PB limping up each step and Maria acting near-catatonic, it fell on Max and Sandra to lug, drag, cajole, and boost them up flight after flight. By the time they reached the roof access door, they were all sweating and gasping air. At least, his hearing had returned.

Max ushered Maria a few feet away and sat her down. "Wait here." He returned to the door and helped Sandra bring PB to a clear section of the roof. They laid him down and inspected his wound.

"I don't want to die," PB said, his voice shivering as much as his body.

Sandra stroked his forehead. "You're not going to die. We'll take good care of you."

"I don't feel so good."

"You got shot. You're not supposed to feel good. But there's a definite exit wound on your back, so that's good. There's no bullet stuck in you that we've got to go fetch. All we've got to do is close you up. So, put your head down and try to think of someplace pleasant. You're in good hands here."

Max wondered if PB could smell Sandra's lies as much as he could. By the look on Drummond's face, even he could tell and he had no sense of smell. "What's it look like down there?" Max asked.

Though he had already surveyed the situation, Drummond floated beyond the edge of the roof and peered down. "Not good. The cops have cleared the area and are waiting for photographers and technicians to come in and analyze the place. I expect they'll start asking questions of neighbors and others to find out what happened. I checked the back exit, and they have a rookie watching there. But even a rookie will notice the four of you. Sorry, but for now, there's no getting down."

"Which means we can't get to a hospital." Sandra moved behind the brick enclosure for the stairwell, and Max and Drummond followed.

"Not so good, huh?" he said.

"Not unless you brought along a needle and thread. It's exactly what I said to him. No bullet to worry about, but we've got to close him up or he'll bleed out long before the police leave here."

Max paced for a brief moment. To Drummond, he asked, "What are they doing with the people who live here?"

"I heard a couple cops saying the folks are going to be given a night in a hotel," Drummond said. "Should be let home tomorrow."

"Then once they're all gone, I can sneak down, break into an apartment, and swipe a needle and thread or bandages or something."

Sandra said, "He'll be dead long before you'll have a chance."

Throwing back his coat, Drummond stuck his hands in his pockets and watched over the boy from several feet in the air. "He's going to be dead if you keep talking about it instead of doing something."

"What about you? Why don't you go down and find a needle and thread?"

"I can try, but I doubt it'll work. Trying to hold something as small as a needle while going through the pain of touching the living world will be near impossible. I mean I can endure a lot, but blinding pain and daintiness don't go together — it's not going to work."

Max and Sandra went back to PB's side. The boy looked pale. When they tried to pull off his shirt, he let out a short yelp. They stopped. With both hands gripping tight, Max took PB's shirt and ripped it open. Again, PB cried out, but Sandra clamped her hand across his mouth.

"Shhh," she said. "If you scream, the police will know somebody's up here. They'll come looking."

PB nodded that he understood as Max tore the loose shirt into two pieces and then balled up each one. Max said, "We're going to plug up those holes with these."

They all knew the hole in the back would hurt the most because they would have to lift his body to reach it. So, Max chose to tackle the entry wound first. He leaned in close. Pumping blood pushed out of the hole like tidewaters on the rocks.

Without giving himself time to back out, Max pressed the shirt onto the wound. PB's body tensed and he screamed. Sandra tried to quiet him, but he wriggled and threw his head aside.

"Stop! Stop!" he cried.

Max let go as if touching an electric wire. With the pressure removed, PB eased back down.

"I'm sorry," he said.

Sandra said, "It's okay. We'll think of something."

"Try this," Max said, and pulled off his coat. "You can bite down and scream into this."

"Okay," PB said. "And I'll still do my best to keep quiet."

Drummond clicked his tongue. "That's one helluva brave kid."

They placed the arm of the coat into PB's mouth and the rest wadded over his face. So that PB knew it was coming, Max announced he was going to try again. He pressed the strip of bloodstained shirt onto the wound and PB screamed. The coat muffled the noise some, but to Max's ears, it still sounded too loud.

More importantly, the shirt soaked up blood but did nothing to stop the bleeding. Max guessed the wound might be too large to simply apply pressure. That seemed to make sense, but then again, he knew nothing about medicine — except not to guess when it came to medicine.

Max threw the shirt away. "Damn."

The boy looked relieved to be done with the pain, but the blood still pulsed out. His eyelids fluttered.

Sandra said, "Hang in there. Don't give up."

Max didn't know if she was talking to him or PB. Probably both.

When Drummond spoke next, Max heard the change in the ghost's tone. A decision had been made — one that Drummond did not take lightly. "I'll do it," he said. "I'll stop the bleeding."

"Can you do that?" Max said. "I mean, I guess it's possible, but wouldn't that take some precise control? So you don't harm the boy?"

"If I don't try, he's not going to make it. Besides, it'll be far easier than trying to keep a needle in my hand, and far more likely to succeed."

"Okay." Max turned to PB. "Hey, can you hear me?"

PB nodded.

"I know you don't believe that I talk with a ghost, that it's all some kind of game between us, but that's wrong. I do see a ghost, and he's here right now. A ghost's touch is cold. Very cold. When he passes through you, you feel a chill. But he can stop and touch you — really touch you — and the more of himself he allows to reach into the living world the colder it gets for you." Max wasn't sure if PB followed, but the boy would believe soon enough.

Sandra said, "We've got to stop that bleeding. We don't have anything hot enough to cauterize the wound. But you can use extreme cold to do the same thing — sort of. It'll be enough to hold you together until we can get you out of here. But it's going to hurt. It'll hurt you and Drummond. A lot. Unlike any pain you've ever had. So, be ready."

To Drummond, Max said, "You sure about this?"

"I've frozen all kinds of things for you guys before. At least this time, I'm doing it to directly save a life."

"I know. Just be careful."

"Thanks for the advice. I was planning on haphazardly throwing myself at the boy, but since you warned me to *be careful*, I'll move with caution."

Oddly, Drummond's sarcasm eased Max's nerves. Knowing the ghost had to lash out gave Max the sense that everything was normal. Of course, trying to keep a teenager from dying on the roof of an apartment building wasn't normal, but it still relaxed Max a small bit.

Drummond put his hand near PB's wound. "Okay. Get that coat ready. This boy's going to scream bloody murder in a second."

Max set the coat in PB's mouth. Chomping like a horse with a bit, PB closed his eyes, wincing in anticipation of the pain. Drummond gave a quick nod and plunged his hand into the boy's shoulder.

The screams of both PB and Drummond melded into an inhuman garble. Tears streamed from PB's eyes as he let his voice rage into the coat. Being a ghost, Drummond didn't have to worry about the police hearing him — his unbridled screams caused Max's skin to shiver.

PB lifted his head. His focus locked on the bullet wound, and Max watched him watch the skin freeze over. Whether from pain, disbelief, or both, the boy's eyes rolled upward and he passed out.

Drummond removed his hands, and for a moment, the only sound Max heard was the wind. Sandra gently moved PB onto his side, and Drummond attacked the exit wound with his ghostly cold hands. He screamed again, but this time he managed to hold back some of the noise.

After pulling his hands away, he said, "That must've been the worst thing I've gone through since becoming a ghost."

"It sounded bad," Max said, "but you've been through worse."

"I don't think so. Something about the kid's skin — it was like a thousand knives slashing into me. Maybe because he's so young. I'm not sure why. But it hurt something awful."

Max thought of his short brush with being a ghost and the nerve-shattering pain he felt when touching the corporeal world. "You've done good," he said.

"I hope." With a weary grin, Drummond drifted over the roof ledge and peered down. "Cops don't look like they're going anywhere soon. I'm taking off for the Other. I'll heal up from this faster in there."

"*Heal?* You're a ghost."

"I can still get hurt. Or did you miss all the screaming?"

"Okay. No need to get snippy. We're not going anywhere until the cops do."

For a reply, Drummond grunted and disappeared. Max slumped down next to Sandra. She had dressed PB in Max's coat and then fallen asleep. Seemed like a good idea to him. He closed his eyes.

Over the next several hours, they rested. Whether asleep or awake, Max's mind tumbled over itself in a jumble of thoughts. He admonished himself for bringing such a dangerous life to two young boys. Then he mocked himself for thinking this was any less dangerous than the lives they had endured before. At least, assuming PB survived, the Sandwich Boys had a shot at a decent life.

Shot? Bad choice of words. Max decided it was good that he could still make a joke — even if only to himself.

His thoughts drifted to Drummond. Max had experienced the ghost world for only a short burst and in a limited way, yet it gave him a new perspective to his old friend. It was lonely being a ghost. No matter how many people Drummond surrounded himself with, he would always be unable to smell or taste or touch. Well, he could touch, but the sensation only brought excruciating pain.

So why does he stay? That bothered Max. Drummond could have moved on to the real afterlife — one that presumably offered more than the cold existence of a ghost — yet he stayed. Max had never bought into Drummond's line that the afterlife was boring and that he preferred to work cases. There had to be more. Thinking on the way Drummond looked at PB, Max wondered if perhaps the answer was simple loneliness.

Except, surely in the afterlife, Drummond would connect with those he knew and loved. Maybe even Patricia Welling, the witch that claimed his heart.

Perhaps the answer was even simpler — fear. Maybe that's what kept most ghosts hanging around. Some of them, of course, had unfinished business to fix, and some had no idea they were even dead. But for the majority, Max thought that they might all be afraid to move on.

As lonely and cold as being a ghost had felt, at least Max knew he had Sandra watching out for him. She brought a sense of warmth into his heart. Maybe Drummond stuck around because working cases with them felt better than leaping into the unknown.

Sitting on the rooftop as the sun descended, Max watched over PB. The boy never stirred. Most of the time, Max checked for the rise and fall of PB's chest.

"Still breathing?" Sandra said in a soft voice.

Max grinned. "Yup. Still breathing."

Nestling under his arm, she hugged his waist. "How about you? Still breathing?"

"They haven't gotten me yet."

Sandra chuckled. "Not for lack of trying."

Max squeezed her shoulder. After a short silence, he said, "I've been trying to make sense of all this."

"Any luck?"

"No."

Her body warmed his side. "It's frustrating. On one hand, we have this cold war turned hot between the Hulls and the Magi Group."

"And that's why Mother Hope caused our accident — to curse you so you'd have to help her."

"Right. Except we also have Cecily Hull in the mix. She's trying to take advantage of this chaos, but she doesn't really know how. So, she tries to make us help her. That much makes sense. It all rather sucks for us, but it makes sense."

"But if she wanted to enlist our help, why with this Libby Holman stuff? It seems unconnected."

"That's the part that bothers me. Cecily Hull does not strike me as an idiot. She could have brought any number of things for us to research that would have helped her out. Heck, all the work I've done checking out the Hull family makes me an expert on them. I probably know Tucker's history far better than Cecily does. That's got to be worth more than the Z. Smith Reynolds murder. But that's what she brings to us."

Sandra lifted her head slightly. "You know what really gets me? If Madame Vansandt told us the truth — which, admittedly, could be a big *If* — but if she did, then which Hull took her eye? And why?"

"That bugs me, too. I mean that's a huge deal — cutting out a person's eye. In a regular case, something like that should click into place right away. I should be saying, 'Oh, of course. They took the eye so that X and Y could happen and that connects to Z and A.' But nothing clicks like that."

"None of this case clicks together."

"Somebody thinks it does. Why else would that pale guy keep being sent after us?"

"Maybe he's not. He was at first, but maybe now we just happen to get in the way."

Max shot up straight, his eyes wide and staring into the dark. "I think you're right. If the Pale Man didn't come here to kill us, then he was sent with his team for something else. While spying on us, Leon found out about it, called Mother Hope, and she told him to fight back. That means two important things: One, the Pale Man definitely works for Tucker Hull. And two, Madame Vansandt has something that everybody wants."

"And she ran."

Max jumped to his feet. He checked over the ledge — only two police cars remained. "I've got an idea. Here's what we need to do. The police should be gone soon. When they leave, you and Maria have to take PB out of here. Go out the back exit. Nobody will see you. Probably nobody left in the building for tonight. The police sent everyone to a hotel so they could investigate. So, you take PB and get him looked at by a doctor.

But no hospitals. Any gunshot wounds showing up will get reported and the police will follow up."

"We'll take care of it. What about you?"

"I'm waiting until Drummond gets back. Then he and I are visiting Madame Vansandt's apartment again. We're going to find whatever caused this shootout."

A thrill surged through Max's body. He had no idea what he would find there, but everything in his gut told him this was the right play. It was a special sensation that he only ever felt from closing in on a solution to a case. And perhaps that was the answer to his question about Drummond. Because what kind of crimes need solving in the afterlife? Maybe this feeling was the real reason Drummond had chosen to stay.

Chapter 15

SANDRA LED HER PART OF THE GROUP out of the building with no trouble. At least, Max knew they did not encounter any police trouble. Any other difficulties that happened, he missed out on. Instead, he sat on the rooftop and waited for Drummond.

An hour later, his partner arrived looking like his old self — dead and pale, but not weary. One police car had returned, so they had to wait on the roof even longer. Without his coat, Max shivered against the night air. An unwelcome wind picked up, forcing him to take shelter in the stairwell.

While Drummond followed the cop around — partially to keep tabs on what the police were doing, partially because the cop was an attractive woman — Max wasted away the time playing Candy Crush on his phone. He had gone over the case details so many times in his head that it all bled together forming a slush of information. Better to clear his mind than wade into that mire once more.

After another hour, Drummond returned. "She's finally leaving."

"What was she doing?"

"Mostly poking around the parking lot and the main floor. I think she's bucking for a promotion and wants to find some key bit of evidence to bolster her chances."

"Because she's poking around downstairs?"

"No, because I overheard her call her boyfriend and tell him that's what she was doing. Oh, and she has a boyfriend."

"So?"

"It's disappointing. Takes the luster off the fantasy."

Max glanced up. "Please, listen to me carefully. I have zero interest in knowing about the sex fantasies of ghosts in general. And I *really* have no interest in knowing yours in particular."

"Then put away your game-phone-thing and let's get to doing what we should be doing."

Max pocketed his phone and headed downstairs. Walking back up the hall felt a little like walking into an old cemetery. The closed doors stood quiet in the still air — tombstones marking long forgotten people. A few bullet holes marred the walls — reminders of the unfortunate deaths from before.

When they reached Madame Vandsandt's apartment, yellow police tape crisscrossed the doorless opening. The splintered jamb had several holes that had been circled and numbered. Max ducked under the tape and entered the apartment.

The main room smelled of officialness. Even if various bullet holes and other detritus had not been marked for evidence, the room would have felt invaded by authority. It stunk the way a hospital stunk — full of special chemicals.

To the right, Max saw an outline where the Pale Man's accomplice had dropped. "Guess he didn't make it."

Drummond hovered over the empty space which should have had markings for the Pale Man but did not. "You better be extra careful. This guy survived and he's going to be angry with you. This is the third time he's failed with you."

"No, he succeeded the first time. He only was supposed to send me to the hospital, which he did. It's these other times that he's screwed up. Frankly, he should be fired. He's not a very good hitman."

"Lucky for you and Sandra."

"Yeah," Max said, losing all sense of humor about the idea. "Let's get to work."

They started in the main room, examining every detail, searching for anything that hinted at being important. Max went to the bookshelves. He pulled out volume after volume of texts with titles that promised riches of magic tutelage. They were all blank.

"None of these books are real."

"Show me," Drummond said, swishing across the air. He looked over Max's shoulder as Max flipped through several books revealing one blank, tattered page after another. "That's not right. Some of those books had words in them. I saw them."

"But you couldn't open them."

"What about the one she used? The one with the spell we need?"

Max dumped the empty books and jumped over to the witch's chair. On the floor was the book of curses — empty. "The spell she cast that let her escape — could it have wiped the books clean?"

Drummond shrugged. "The one constant I've learned about magic is never assume you know the limit of the stuff. Every single time I think I understand that world, along comes a witch who outdoes my highest expectations."

Pulling on his lip, Max walked off to the kitchen. While he accepted Drummond's notion that the world of witches sunk deeper than they knew, he also believed there were limitations. After all, every witch Max had encountered had to use certain ingredients and go through a casting process. It wasn't as if they could learn to spew lasers from their eyes. That wasn't how it worked. Magic had rules just like physics. It wasn't a trick.

Unless, this time, it was.

"What if it was like a magic trick?" he said. When nobody answered, he glanced up to find that Drummond had gone into a different room to search. Max took a seat at the kitchen table — a small rectangular slab of wood pressed against one wall. Dead flowers stuck out of a cloudy vase.

If it had been a trick, it was one that involved actual magic — a *magic* magic trick. It could have been done like the old child's trick of writing with lemon juice as "invisible ink". All those texts could have been written in some special ink that reacted by going blank whenever a specific spell was cast. That would also account for the fact that most of these texts were impossible to find. What a great way to pass on history and spells and all their learning without being persecuted by those who don't agree — something witches knew a lot about.

He had no idea if he was right, but Max felt better knowing he had any idea at all. He stepped up to the kitchen counter and searched through the utensil drawers, the deep cabinets of pots and pans, and the overhead cabinets with canned foods and cereal boxes. On the splashboard behind the oven sat an egg-timer shaped like an egg with two big eyes and a silly smile. Next to a coffee maker was a mug with the words "WORLD'S BEST GRANDMA!" written on the side. Nothing appeared out of the ordinary, though Max shuddered at the thought of Madame Vansandt having a grandchild.

Drummond's strong voice cut through the quiet apartment. "Hey, Max, in here."

Max found the ghost in the master bedroom. A more modern-looking room than any other in the apartment, the bedroom had a sterile aspect about it that brought to mind a hotel room. There were pictures on the wall and a dresser and a television, but none of it connected to a specific personality. The main room with its tapestries and old books and dim lights — that screamed of the old witch. But this bedroom looked generic. Which made Max wonder which version of Madame Vansandt was the truth — this room or the other one?

"You're not going to believe this one," Drummond said, gesturing to the bedside table.

Max saw a book sitting under a modern lamp. Picking it up, he read the cover — *Cabbages and Kings* by O. Henry. The Magi Group named themselves after O. Henry's *The Gift of the Magi*, and O. Henry had some tangential connections with them.

He set the book back. "That's weird, but not enough. Lots of people have this book. She could've been a fan. Or she could've been getting to know her enemy."

"Or she could be working with them."

Max opened a small drawer built into the bedside table. A pencil rolled atop a small pad. Next to the pad were two leather-bound, pocket-sized books — *Roads of Destiny* and *Whirligigs* both by O. Henry. Max opened *Roads of Destiny*. On the dedication page, he found a handwritten inscription—

To Mrs. Vansandt —
The Magi welcome you

"Crap," Max muttered and displayed the book for Drummond.

"That pretty much settles it. She's part of the Magi Group."

"Not necessarily."

"Max, c'mon. One book might've been a coincidence. But three of them and one is inscribed to her from the Magi? For Pete's sake, didn't the guy only put out three books? She has them all. She's part of that group."

"I know what it looks like, but think about it. Does it make any sense? If Madame Vansandt worked with the Magi, then why haven't they used her? Why go to all that trouble with me when she could have cast the spell herself? I mean, she's clearly got some mean mojo. From what we've seen of her, don't you think if she teamed up with Mother Hope, they could have taken out Tucker Hull without all this cursing nonsense?"

"That's a bit thin. Yes, she's powerful, but we don't know how powerful. We also don't know how well she gets along with Mother Hope. In my experience, witches care a lot about the pecking order. Mother Hope may have brought her into the Magi fold, but I doubt they were too close. You're also forgetting one important thing."

"Which is?"

"Mother Hope had it in for you. Her method here may not be the most efficient, but a witch can get blinded by her hatred. So much so that she'll convince herself hurting you is the best way to hurt the Hulls and achieve her goals. I've seen it before."

"Maybe," Max said, staring at the book. "But look around. You see anything else here that looks like Magi? If I'm going to believe any real connection with that group, I'd have to suspect Madame Vansandt is a freelancer. Possibly did some work for the Magi and that's why she got this book with the ..."

Max flipped to the inscription again. Drummond came in close, his eyes on Max. "What is it, pal? I can see your wheels turning."

"The inscription. It's here."

"Yeah, it is. That's why we're talking about this. Right?"

"I mean, it's here in this book. Why didn't it get wiped clean like all the other books? Not the text of the book, but the inscription. If she was really part of the Magi group, and this spell she used wiped away all the secrets, then why didn't she protect this as well?"

"Because she's not with them. Somebody put this here for us to find."

Max's pulse quickened. He put the book back. "Somebody wants us to conclude that Madame Vansandt is with the Magi. Which brings us to the next questions — why? and who?"

"Well, let's think about it." As Drummond spoke, he floated through the bed. "If these books are intended to set up the witch in a false connection, that means they had to be planted for us to find. So, somebody had to know we'd be coming here."

"Then it couldn't have been done before today. We had no idea we'd be here before that. Heck, we'd never even heard of this witch until last night."

"Once we got here, there was no chance to sneak those books in. The only person I saw go into this room was your wife's friend, Maria."

"You think her being afraid and all was an act? She's really a mole for the Magi or someone else?"

Drummond threw out the notion with a toss of his hand. He had drifted half-in a wall but took no notice. "We've both seen enough fear to know that was the real thing."

"Unless she's a really good actress."

"Sorry, but I don't believe it. Maria was Vansandt's student. She would know about the disappearing words on the pages. If for some reason she wanted to set up her mentor, she would know better than to try it this way. Besides, you're forgetting that there was a simple way to get the books in under our noses."

Max rubbed his eyes. His brain felt foggy from lack of sleep. "You got me. What am I missing?"

"We were up on the roof for hours. Anybody could have come in here during that time."

"You're right. All those involved in this would know that people would come back at some point. Especially us. We're the research crew. Of course, we'd be expected to return here and figure out what's going on. So, somebody plants these books and waits for us to go down the wrong path. Somebody who knows we'd look at the books. Unless ... uh-oh."

Drummond froze. "Unless this was meant as lure to get us wasting time in the bedroom while our enemies took up positions in the living room. Stay here. I'll check."

Though Drummond dashed out and back in seconds, Max already knew the answer. He walked out of the bedroom to find Leon Moore sitting in the old witch's chair.

Leon opened his arms wide like a conqueror. "I knew you couldn't resist coming back here."

Chapter 16

DRUMMOND BOLTED AHEAD, his hands turning icy white as he speared towards Leon. Two feet before he struck, Drummond was thrown aside and slammed into the bookshelves. He bellowed as the wood cracked and dust puffed out. Though unable to hear the ghost, Leon noticed the wood and dust.

From under his shirt, Leon pulled out his necklace — a ward against ghosts. "Your friend doesn't learn. I never talk with you unprepared."

Max put his hands in his pockets and leaned against the wall. "I guess he's an optimist when it comes to hurting you."

Leon laughed hard enough to cough, bending over slightly in the process. For an instant, he looked like the man Max had first met a few years ago — an old librarian harboring a love for books and research and concerned only with the pursuit of knowledge. But as the coughing subsided, Leon straightened, and the new man returned — a guard and lackey of Mother Hope doing all that she asked in return for strength and vitality. Max wondered what else Leon had to give in order to gain his temporary youth.

"Please step a little closer. We have a bit to talk about," Leon said, "and I don't want your optimist getting in my way. So, pardon the magic."

He bent down and flicked open a lighter. Setting it close to the floor, the flame ignited a thin line of dark powder Max had failed to spot earlier. The flame shot forward, following the line of powder like a racecar on a straight track. It sped by Drummond, made a right angle turn near the front door and continued on. Another right angle and it was headed for Max.

He knew enough magic to step forward rather than play chicken — especially when he noticed that the line went right underneath him. It finished where it began, having formed a large square around Max and Leon.

Drummond pounded on the air above the line as if it were made of thick, solid glass. "I hate when they do that to me. I'm here for you, pal, but I can't get in there."

Max nodded. This wasn't the first time magic had been used to keep Drummond away.

Leon returned to the witch's chair. "That's better. Now we won't be interrupted."

"Can we get this over with? Or I'll start feeling as optimistic as the ghost."

Leon's mirth dropped away leaving an inscrutable glare upon his black, leathered face. "I suppose I should forgive your rudeness. You're a Northerner, after all. You weren't brought up right."

"You know, ever since I moved down here, all of you people have been telling me how rude I am, but I'm not the one constantly trying to take over, I'm not the one kidnapping people, and I'm certainly not the one making deals with a witch for a false sense of youth."

"You have no clue what you're talking about. Which is why I'm here and you haven't been hurt. Yet. I want you — Mother Hope wants you — to understand the situation in its fullest."

"I'm really not in the mood for threats I'm just going to ignore."

Drummond clapped his hands. "That's right! Give him a hard time."

"No threats," Leon said, crossing his legs. "Well, not yet. Let's start with some simple truth. You see, you seem to think that we can all live without Mother Hope. But to do so means letting the Hulls run things, and that is a dangerous, unthinkable existence."

"I don't want that at all. I don't want any of you people running anything. There's no need."

"There absolutely is. Power always exists, and if we don't

control it, then someone else will. It's very much like politics. We, all of us, need to have somebody in charge. It makes me think of those people who get their hackles all raised up about government. They don't want government around. Government's the problem. Don't let the government take control of this or that because they'll screw it up like everything they do.

"But the truth is that they do want government — for without a government, we'd have anarchy, and that is not sustainable. So, no matter how much they complain, and they love to complain, people do want a government — just not for the same purpose as you. One side thinks the government should provide education and health care. One side thinks it should provide military and security. They all want it, and they all don't want it.

"Our situation is the same. Somebody will take authority over the use of magic in this city and in this state, maybe even in this country. That can't be changed. We need that authority just as we need a government. Since you seem to act like a swing vote, you have found yourself in a unique, temporary position. You can throw your support to either side and help choose all of our fates."

Max wagged his finger. "Nice speech, but let's be honest about this. I don't really get to choose anything."

"Oh, no, you're wrong about that." Leon popped from his chair, but Max caught a slight crinkle at the corner of his eyes as though the move hurt a little — perhaps Mother Hope's magic hadn't made the man as young as he had hoped. Leon stepped in close, blocking Max's view of Drummond. "I need you to pay attention. I'm not here out of some misguided loyalty. I'm here because I've convinced the Magi Group to give you a chance to do the right thing. The others, especially Mother Hope, are livid at what you've done. They want to use the curse you still have on you and watch as you spend eternity stuck between the living and the dead. But I've seen you work. You're a smart man. All you need is the facts and a chance. You'll make the right decision."

"Your confidence in me is astounding. I'd probably be more impressed if I wasn't standing in the rubble of a witch's apartment while my partner is blocked from joining us."

Leon inched back. "I do have to protect myself."

"He's right," Drummond said. "If I could get to him, I'd make him sorry."

"Don't let these precautions distract you. Instead, please, think this through."

"I have," Max said.

"Really? Because for a long time, over a century now, the Hull family has had a lock on their power in this area. Nobody could beat them. If you were a witch, if you dabbled in the mystic arts, or even if you performed the most meaningless of spells, they knew about it, and they either allowed it or they visited you and made you aware of their rules. Forty years ago, to be a witch in North Carolina was much like being a serf in a monarchy. You lived your life and hoped not to fall under the gaze of the Duke or the King or whoever owned you. You tried to follow the Royal family's rules, but they often rewrote those rules at a whim."

"I get the picture."

"What you fail to see, though, is that it's all changed. Bringing you and your wife to the South started it. Since your arrival, you have bested them. More than once. And that has weakened their stronghold around here. Now is the time to strike."

Max rolled his eyes, making sure Leon saw his expression. "I've heard all of this from Mother Hope. Repeating doesn't make it so."

"But it is so. It's the truth."

Drummond flew around to the front door attempting to get a better view. "That guy wouldn't know the truth if it stood up and bit him."

"Okay, I'll play along for a moment." Max strolled to the witch's chair and plopped down, sticking one leg over the armrest. He grinned inwardly at Leon's visible discomfort. "Let's say I go along with all of this. I free Dr. Connor from her curse and somehow you convince her to destroy Tucker Hull. All that goes as you plan and then what? Who takes over? Mother Hope? I'm sure she'd like that kind of power."

"Who else is there?" Leon scoffed. "You can't seriously be considering Cecily Hull?"

"I'm not considering anybody. This is all hypothetical."

Leon paused and drummed his fingers on the back of his head. "Mother Hope said you'd never co-operate. She said no matter what I presented to you, that you would still find reasons to doubt me. I should learn to listen to her more. She's always right."

"Sorry to disappoint. But I don't think you should go around saying *she's always right*. She's been wrong about me many times."

"We'll see." Leon moved in front of Max. When Max tried to stand, Leon shoved him back in the seat. "She said you would be rude and obstinate. She said you would refuse to help us. She was right about all of that. But she also told me how to make you help us."

"Should I bother asking or will you simply tell me? Oh, I know, let me guess. Either I help the Magi Group with their Dr. Connor problem or you are going to kill me."

"No. Sadly. That would've been much easier. No, if you refuse to help us, I've been ordered to kill your wife."

"You sonofa —" Max launched off the chair with his fist flying.

Leon sidestepped. "She said you'd try to hit me."

"Lay a hand on my wife and I'll kill you all."

"Don't put me in that position, then. Find Dr. Connor's body, free her from the curse, and let the world return to a semblance of balance. That's all we want."

"And if I don't, you'll kill Sandra?"

"I'll do my best to make it quiet and painless. Then I'll send you to follow her."

Chapter 17

MAX SPENT THE NIGHT IN HIS CAR. He parked in the empty lot of a defunct strip mall, leaned his seat back, and shut his eyes. His mind, however, refused to be shut off. Despite the chatter in his head, he managed to get a few hours of rest. The remainder of the night, he worked out their next steps.

As dawn approached, he sent messages to Sandra via Drummond. They agreed that they couldn't meet at the warehouse. Too much traffic going in and out of an abandoned tobacco warehouse would get noticed. Sandra suggested the Forsyth Public Library, and Max liked the idea. Drummond wanted nothing to do with another library, so he went back to the Other to finish healing and to check on Dr. Connor.

Serving all of Forsyth County, the public library was on West 5th Street in downtown Winston-Salem — roughly seven blocks from their office. Max drove away from the city before doubling back. He entered a paid parking structure and headed out on foot. Two cabs and several blocks of walking gave him the hope that he had ditched anybody following him.

"How's PB?" he asked Sandra as they settled in a back corner of the library's references section.

"Resting. He's with Maria, and she promised to keep good care of him. She's looking better, too. Starting to come back to reality."

"Where is he? What doctor did you get? He'll be okay, right?"

"He's fine. He's staying at Maria's house."

"Her house? You can't put him there. Or her, for that matter. You know we're being watched. We can't —"

"Stop," she said and waited for him to close his mouth. The library was mostly empty so early in the morning, but not entirely. Max wondered if Sandra had suggested this location because she knew he'd be forced to control his mouth. She went on, "I know you're worried about PB and everything that's going on, but it's not all on you. I know exactly what our situation is, and I made the call."

"But —"

"No. You listen. I had to get that boy stable and taken care of, and just because you said to go get a doctor who wouldn't report a gunshot wound, doesn't make it happen. I don't know any doctors like that. I'm sure they're around, but if I did what you wanted, then by the time I found a doctor, approached and convinced that person I'm not a cop and I really needed help, and then got that doctor to wherever I left everybody, PB would've been dead. So, I decided to go to Maria's because it solved our problems. Being in her home would calm her down and get her thinking again. She would have a needle, thread, and ways to sterilize the needle — all easy to find because it's her home. And I was right. She pulled it together, got what we needed, and I sewed PB up. He's resting, watching some TV, and lapping up Maria's attempts at mothering. Before you start in about them being watched, they are both minor enough in all of this to be left alone."

"You don't think the Hulls will snag them to use as leverage against us?"

"Not with everything else that's going on. In another situation, I'd worry. But if the Hulls or even Mother Hope attempted a kidnapping, they'd be exposing themselves to attack from the other side. Not to mention that I will put a curse on them which will never be broken."

Max's muscles tensed and his pulse tapped at the back of his head. "Don't say that."

"What? That I'd curse them?"

"You need to back off the magic, hon. You're not a witch, and you shouldn't become one. I'm sorry. I know you've enjoyed learning about it all, but that was research to help us in our fights against witches. You can't start being one. It's a dangerous road."

Sandra placed a hand on his knee. "Honey, that's sweet, but you don't need to worry. I've got the whole thing covered. Besides, I've not had many friends or really much of a life since we moved down here. At least now, I've got Maria."

"Remember what Madame Vansandt said to Maria. Witchcraft is a Pandora's Box, and you are on the verge of opening it."

Sandra leaned in and looked Max sharp in the eyes. "I'm fine."

He had heard that tone many times before. It meant *shut up because I'm not changing my decision*. So, he kissed her cheek. "Okay, hon. No problem." That meant *you're wrong but I don't want to fight now*.

"So, what's next?" Sandra said, implying she knew he had planned something. With that simple question, both of them felt better and let their "almost" argument float away. It wasn't dead, though. They knew there would be a time for that fight, but they had higher priorities at the moment.

Max glanced at all the books. "Research."

"Good. We can find Dr. Connor's body and be done with this."

"No. Not yet. First, we're going to find Madame Vansandt's eye. We need it for leverage. We need it desperately."

"What can I do to help?"

"Go find Jammer J and get him to PB. The poor kid must be a wreck of worry."

"I doubt that. Those kids are tough."

"Still, Jammer J will want to be there for PB. After you've got that done, I'll need you to do their job today. Follow Mother Hope around. See if she does anything pertinent to our case."

"Okay."

"No matter what, don't get involved in anything you see Mother Hope doing. Just write down what happened and let me know."

"You got it."

"I'm serious. There's a real threat from all these enemies. Don't let them know you're watching them."

With a mock salute, Sandra said, "Aye aye, Cap'in!"

As she hugged him, Max had a strange, cold sensation wash over him — one that had only happened a few times in his life. The thought flashed in his head — *this is the page turning.* He had experienced that same sensation, that same thought, the day he proposed to Sandra. He had experienced it again the day he took the job that brought him to North Carolina. On those occasions, he understood why he felt that way. Life was turning to a new chapter. It was exciting, adventurous, and full of promise.

But this — this terrified him.

Chapter 18

As usual in Max's life, the only real option was to keep moving forward. That meant packing away his fears to focus on his research. Lucky him, he sat in a library.

Though the situation had complexity, there was really only one missing component to all of it, only one thing that constantly stood out as a mystery — ZSRLH. Cecily Hull had brought that to them when she could have taken it to any of her own people. Why? Max liked to think it was because he had the reputation of being the best, except that did not seem likely. She brought it to him; she had a reason.

He tried to put himself in her shoes. She had been actively working to destroy Tucker Hull so that she could take over the family business. She knew this code was important and that it somehow held a big secret. Perhaps she didn't trust those who work under her. Not with something this important.

"But then why the bull story about hacking family computers?" Max whispered to himself. Could be that she simply didn't want anybody to know the truth — not that the truth was damaging but rather that the more cards she held to her chest, the more control she had over a precarious situation.

And she knew we were being watched. Max leaped to his feet and headed into the stacks. Of course. It wasn't by accident that she visited Sandra on the same night as Mother Hope. She knew all about Max's curse and had to act fast.

It was just as Leon had said — somebody had to hold the power. With Tucker appearing to be weakened, she had to make her moves, too. Even if she could trust her own people, she still had to employ Sandra and Max — they were her best chance of solving things before her enemies. She had to force them into a position between her and Mother Hope or risk Mother Hope getting full control.

Max trailed his fingers along the spines of books until he found the one he wanted — a biography of Libby Holman. "Nobody's controlling us," he said and rushed to a table to work through the book again — particularly going over the chapters regarding the murder of Z. Smith Reynolds.

He spent two hours checking and re-checking each fact, each detail, and each opinion presented in the case. Nothing jumped out as new or unexpected. Nowhere could he find that nugget of information that would shine like the sun breaking through stormy clouds. None of the texts helped.

Texts? He resisted the urge to smack his forehead. Instead, he quietly placed the books back where he had found them in the stacks and sat at one of the public access computers. He brought up Google and clicked on *Images*.

Pictures had often helped him discover a breakthrough. Photographs and paintings were often a more reliable historical record than texts. Too many people tried to rewrite history by actually rewriting the texts. But the photos and paintings — those often told the truth. Even in the modern world of Photoshop, Max found that images of a world, when taken as a group rather than individually, created a clearer picture of history than any single eyewitness account. Witness memories were notoriously flawed.

He started as broadly as possible by typing "images of Z Smith Reynolds and Libby Holman" into the search bar. Two seconds later, he scrolled through thousands of photographs, portraits, and other images. There were playbills from Libby's Broadway days as well as album covers and other notices of her work in the entertainment industry. There were pictures of the actual 45s with Libby's name on the label and photos of her on stage dressed to dazzle. Z. Smith had plenty of his own, too — particularly, photographs of him standing in front of one airplane or another.

Max narrowed the search down to the years 1931 through

1933. Smith's murder was in 1932, so Max thought it best to pick up the year before and after as well. Sure enough, plenty of images flooded the screen — many of them from old newspapers, most of them regarding the murder and Libby's legal troubles afterward.

Clicking through page after page, inspecting each photo carefully, Max was not surprised when he hit the photo five pages deep. It jumped out at him, and he knew instantly this was what he had wanted to find. Clicking on the photo enlarged it and added the caption — *Libby Holman with close friend, 1933.* It depicted the widow sitting on the patio of somebody's home. She had dressed down and wore a somber expression, but none of that captured Max's interest. The woman standing behind Libby had stopped Max's search — the woman wearing the eye patch.

She was a tall woman, her head nearly cut out of the photo, and she looked forward as if able to see through the camera, through the photo, directly at Max. That look bothered him — it tickled the back of his thoughts. He had seen that look before.

"Has to be in one of the books," he said. He blasted out of his chair and hurried back down the stacks to where he had left the Libby Holman biographies. Flipping through, he reached the middle section with glossy photos.

His mouth dried as his pulse quickened. He knew he would find it. After years of researching things, he knew the taste of victory.

In the second book on the third page of photographs, he found it. Z. Smith Reynolds, his new wife, Libby, and four friends all draped on furniture by an enormous fireplace. Sitting bolt upright in the middle of one couch, that same tall woman glared directly through the photo — except in this image, she had both eyes. According to the caption, her name was Marlyn Chester.

He checked the date and clapped the book shut. "Got it!"

A few minutes on the computer revealed that Marlyn Chester had lived her entire life in North Carolina, settling in

High Point around 1955. She had a husband and a daughter, and she died in 1972 on her sixtieth birthday. The husband died shortly after, and the daughter, Candice, inherited the house. Further searching showed that Candice still owned the property.

"Probably still lives there, too," Max said as he copied down the address.

He got in his car and hopped on Route 74 South straight through High Point. Candice lived on the southern end of the city in a cluster of homes nestled near the junction of Routes 74 and 85. Though next to the highway, the area felt secluded owing to the tall grass lots and copious trees that broke up the view. The sound of traffic could not be masked completely, but the location seemed better off than Max had expected.

Candice Chester's home, a single-story rancher, sat on a small rise with a narrow driveway. When Max walked up to a screened-in porch, he had the sensation of being watched — not the surveillance feeling that dogged him everywhere he went, but rather he thought Candice observed his approach. He rang the doorbell once and she opened as if she had been posed to open it all along.

Like her mother, Candice had the height to make her a good basketball player. She shared her mother's stern glower, too. "What do you want?" she asked. Despite her imposing posture, her light Southern voice lessened the abruptness of her tone.

"Ms. Chester, my name is Max Porter, and if you'll give me a few minutes, I'd like to ask you some questions about your mother."

"My momma?"

"I do research for people, and some of my work brought up your mother's name. Please, I'll only be short time."

"No. Good day, Mr. Porter."

As she closed the door, Max blurted out, "Would you like to know how your mother lost her eye?"

Candice paused. "What kind of research are you doing, exactly?"

He saw it clear on her face — she already knew most of the

story. If she hadn't, he would have seen curiosity or concern. But instead of pushing further, asking what he knew or why he thought he knew anything, she countered with a question of her own — one that would reveal more about himself than provide any answers.

He considered trying to be charming or thoughtful or even threatening. However, his gut told him that none of those approaches would work. Instead, he decided to use a tactic Drummond had taught him long ago. He called it *the truth*.

"Ms. Chester, you have a choice to make. You can let me in and talk this through with me, or you can turn me away. But I'm not the only person looking into all of this. I just happen to be the best, so I'm here first. Soon enough, the rest will follow. Ask yourself this: do you want to work with me — a guy who simply is looking for answers and poses no threat to you — or do you want to work with the Hulls?"

She shoved open the creaking screen door and gestured to two cushioned chairs on the porch. "You want some sweet tea?"

"No, thank you."

Though he could tell she had no interest in serving him tea of any kind, he also saw that, like a classic Southern gal, she was insulted he had refused her offer. But no matter how many times he gave it a try, Max could not get used to sweet tea — a concoction that was one part iced tea and ten parts sugar. Still, he could imagine what Drummond would say — *Take the tea. Drink it, if you have to. But whatever you do, don't insult the person you want to get something from.*

She sat in the chair to his left, crossed her legs and arms, and set her jaw firm. Even sitting, she towered above him. "I'm listening."

Stick to the main point. Both Max's brain and Candice's body language screamed the message home. "No doubt, you already know your mother was good friends with Libby Holman."

"Great friends."

"Did they meet before she married Z. Smith Reynolds or were they introduced through Reynolds?"

"Does it matter?"

"Not really. Just the researcher in me trying to get all the blanks filled in."

Her thumb bounced a rhythm on her arm. "Then you're wasting my time."

"Wait, wait. I'm sorry." Max wanted to smack himself — *stick to the point!* "I wanted to lay the groundwork, but I see that's not necessary. You obviously knew your mother quite well."

"My momma was very special." Candice glanced to a photo on the wall — Marlyn, with her eye-patch sitting on the porch in the same seat Max occupied.

"She certainly was. She touched many lives, but none more than Libby. Like you said, they were the greatest of friends — the kind that would do anything for each other."

"You have a point, or do you like telling people things they already know?"

"That's the point right there — that you already know this. All of it. You know exactly the story I'm about to say, but you're going to make me say it anyway."

Pulling her shoulders back, Candice appeared to gain another few inches. "You're not the first to come here thinking they know something about my mother and Libby and the murder of Z. Smith Reynolds. But I'll tell you this — nobody has ever figured it all out. So, nobody ever gets what they come here for."

Max scooted onto the edge of his chair. He leaned over, resting his elbows on his knees. "Well, then, allow me to take a crack at this."

"I'm assuming, since you're here, that you know what my momma was."

"Yes, she was a witch."

"Then it shouldn't shock you that she taught me a few things. I never followed the path and became a full witch, but I did learn enough to make you sorry — if need be."

"You can make any threat you want. I know the truth, so your threats won't ever be used."

She ran her tongue across her teeth as she thought. "Go ahead, Mr. Porter. Let me hear what you think my momma did and did not do."

"Your mother, Marlyn Chester, loved Libby Holman. They were close friends, and I'd wager that Marlyn considered Libby a sister. Now, Libby married well, and all seemed fine except that she and Smith were having difficulties getting pregnant. At some point, Marlyn offered to help. I'm not sure if Libby knew that Marlyn was a witch, not at that moment, but it was not something a sister needed to hide."

Candice did not speak, but she made an involuntary nod. Max caught it and the small gesture bolstered his confidence.

"Except Libby turned her down. Marlyn got upset and Libby got angry. There were many pictures that showed Libby with your mother — though, mostly she kept to the sides or the back. But then there's a gap. Six long months in which the photos stopped. I suspect they hardly spoke to one another. Until the Fourth of July party when Libby invited Marlyn to try to patch things up. What had changed? Libby was pregnant. She had a problem, too. She was nervous to tell Smith about the baby. They had been trying and failing for so long, and he had recently become controlling and jealous. She insisted that she was loyal to him, but he saw philandering everywhere. Particularly with their permanent house guest, Albert Walker. How am I doing?"

Candice held still, locking her eyes on him. "Mr. Porter, I am not going to hold your hand through all of this. Finish your story or leave."

"At the party, Libby makes up with Marlyn and then asks for help. Would Marlyn cast a spell to ease Smith's mind? This was a bigger favor than Libby realized because Marlyn did not like Smith at all. I'd even say she hated Smith."

"Oh? What makes you think so?"

"All those photographs with Libby — rarely was Smith anywhere to be found. On the few occasions your mother and Smith are together, you can see their discomfort. In fact, in a few photos, the daggers shooting from her eyes are unmistakable. And, of course, they would be enemies. Smith did not approve of the friendship, and as far as your mother was concerned, she would never allow anything to break apart her sisterhood with Libby."

Candice raised an eyebrow. "Go on."

"The night of the party, everybody was drinking. By most accounts, people regularly were going off into the woods — presumably to —"

"Yes, I know what they were doing."

Clearing his throat, Max said, "Of course. Well, um, Libby was seen going off into the woods, too. Smith was heard later yelling about that fact. The thing is — nobody really knows what went on with Libby in the woods. She said she was merely walking around, clearing her head, that kind of thing. Albert denies any wrongdoing, though according to others at the party, he was also missing for quite some time. Now, most people assumed they were having an affair."

"But you don't."

"If you look, even a cursory glance at Libby Holman's life, that behavior doesn't add up. She was wild and impulsive and all of that, but she wasn't cruel. To cheat on Smith right under his nose, in the middle of a party full of friends, that's too much to believe."

Candice's eyes twitched as if she held back a knowing smile. "Tell me what you think happened."

"I think it's quite clear to anybody who knows that witches and spells are real. Libby goes off into the woods for a walk and she comes upon Marlyn. They chat. Perhaps Marlyn offers her one last chance to make up for real — leave Smith and return to New York — something like that. But Libby has a baby on the way and wants Marlyn to help with calming Smith. That's all. Marlyn agrees and Libby leaves the woods.

"Now, I'm no expert on witchcraft, I don't know all the depths of the spells and curses and such, but a spell to calm a husband would be an easy task. Yet we have photographic evidence that Marlyn cast a very serious, very dark spell. One that required a witch's eye. I suspect, after Libby left the woods,

Marlyn went a different route with her magic. She probably wanted to curse Smith, but going up against the entire Reynolds family would be suicide. And her anger at Libby, her sense of betrayal, had never left. Witches are not known for easy forgiveness. I think she cursed Libby — a curse that would start with Smith's death and continue throughout Libby's life, ending only when she committed suicide. Even then, considering the dark nature of the curse and the sacrifice required to cast it, perhaps the poor woman is still cursed."

When Max finished, Candice sat without saying a word. He heard only the creak of her chair and an occasional heavy sigh. Experience and Drummond had taught him to stay quiet. Wait it out. Anything he said now would ruin whatever chances he had of gaining information.

At length, Candice covered her heart with her long fingers. "Congratulations, Mr. Porter. You are the first to ever put all the pieces together."

"Not all. I still don't know what spell she cast."

"Neither do I. She tried to get me to follow the path of magic, but as a teen, I rebelled against her life and wanted nothing to do with that world. Spells like the one she gave up an eye for — well, I never learned that kind of thing."

Tilting his head down, Max frowned. "I see. Then I'm sorry to have bothered you. I had hoped that by knowing the spell, I would have been able to connect that magic with another situation. I guess I was wrong."

"Stay here," Candice said as she went inside. A few moments later, she returned with a small canister like a soup thermos. "In her later years, as her health declined, my momma told me the story of Libby. It was important to her that I know, that I understood, because it was her single greatest regret. She also told me that over the years to come, people would suspect her involvement and they would come here. They would want this container, and I was not to give it to anybody except the one who came to share the story, the full story, and who did not seek this out."

"I don't follow. What's in that?"

She traced the top with her finger. "You being here — not just here at my home, but here in Winston-Salem, in North Carolina — it's no accident. Sometimes I remember when I was little and my momma would explain the universe to me. Where other children were told tales of a god who watched from above, my momma taught me of the way the universe worked like a bizarre clock — each piece precise and important to the running of the whole. Magic, she would say, was nothing more than the ability to open the clock's face and tinker with a few of the gears. Good magic made the clock work better, stronger. The other kind, the bad magic, attempted to force the clock to change its time or the way it ran. She taught me all about the Hulls and the Magi and the way that together, the two groups formed a balance. When that balance was upset, it was like throwing a wrench into the clock."

Max leaned back, his face open wide. "You know, don't you? All about what's going on here."

"Of course, I know. I've watched, I've listened, and I've waited. I knew there would be visitors all looking for this container. But I see now that my momma was right. The universe is a delicate clock, always looking for the right balance. That's why I say you are here, no mistake about it."

"I'm sorry, but I don't believe in destiny or Fate or anything like that."

"Don't have to. I know that you are the one she wanted to have this." Candice handed the container over.

It wasn't heavy, and he could feel that it was filled with liquid. "Do I open it?"

"No. Not until you're ready to use it."

"You still haven't told me what's in it or what it's for."

Looking down at him like an impatient teacher, she said, "It's from a witch. What do you think it is? Magic, of course. Powerful magic. Powerful enough to free my momma from the imbalance she created so long ago. Use it when there is no other option. You only get to do it once, so be sure."

"I will. I promise."

Candice closed her eyes and a slow smile crept onto her

face. "Thank you. Good luck. Good bye."

As Max opened the screen door, he paused. The fog in his mind had begun to clear, revealing how many of the parts in this case linked up. Acting on instinct, he turned back. "I have one last question, but it's very important."

"If I can help, I will."

"It's about before your mother was married."

After getting an answer, Max walked to his car. He couldn't help but skip a tiny step or two. Things looked like they might be turning around. He placed the canister in his coat pocket and pulled out his cell phone.

He called Cecily Hull, and by way of greeting, he said, "We need to talk."

Chapter 19

As Max shoved down the last bite of greasy pizza, he decided the Hanes Mall food court had been a bad choice of meeting place. He should have known that Cecily would be late out of spite and that he would start eating to curb his nervous energy. With his stomach gurgling its disagreement, he tapped his feet. He had nothing to do but wait and smell the other foods his tense bowels had no desire to experience at the moment.

On the plus side, the food court was public. The lunch hour had gone but plenty of people still hung around which provided Max with some important advantages. He could feel relatively safe during their meeting — not that she planned him harm, but he knew others were watching. If she had a big move to make, it would not happen there. Neither would those watching take a chance at any kind of strike — too public. Of course, they had no problem shooting up a downtown apartment building, so perhaps Max's assessment needed refinement.

More importantly, Cecily would not like to be in any food court. If his plan could succeed, he needed her off-balance.

The controlled, steady rhythm of Cecily's walk announced her arrival seconds before he saw her approach. A well-dressed man with a long, pock-marked face accompanied her. With nothing more than a movement of her head, he took up a position far enough back as to be unobtrusive but close enough that he could jump in should Max attempt anything stupid.

Don't you know me? Max thought. *I'm full of stupid.*

"Something amusing?" Cecily asked as she went to sit, saw something on the chair not to her liking, and pulled over a different chair.

"Sorry that this isn't the kind of place you normally eat at."

"I won't be dining." She caught herself fidgeting in the chair, and with a single breath, she crossed her legs and eased back as if this had been her office chair for years. Max had never seen a person switch into such a commanding role with so little motion. Through flattened lips, she said, "Do you have something to tell me or am I here to observe your inability to get food into your mouth?"

Max grabbed a napkin and wiped around his mouth. He felt a splotch of tomato sauce smear off. *Great. Ten seconds in and I've already lost control of this.* Except he had a lot more on his side than posturing, and the time had come to go on the offensive.

"You're right," he said. "Let's get started. For us, it all begins with you bringing a string of letters to my wife — ZSRLH. Where did you find that? And please, save us both the embarrassment of pretending to buy into your hacker story."

Cecily rolled her shoulder and looked away, her tight mouth drawing even tighter. "Your firm was hired to find out what that code meant, not how I acquired it."

"Except that oftentimes where information came from will clue us in to its meaning. Besides, you should know better than to lie to me after I've done my research. Where did you get the code?"

"This is not an information exchange. You report to me, not the other way around."

"Yet if you withhold —"

"Enough. Tell me what you found or I will leave."

Max saw that the man standing a few feet away had puffed up and taken a step closer. Pushing out a smile, Max turned his palms up. "Why are we arguing? We're on the same side, right? I was only trying to get a fuller picture, but you're correct. You are the client, and I don't need to know anything more than what I was assigned to research. I'm sorry."

"Apology accepted." She dropped her hand to the side and her bodyguard stepped back. "Now, let me hear your report."

He paused long enough to see her squirm in her seat. To

anybody looking, she would have simply been shifting a little, but Max knew better. She would never have shown the slightest change if she weren't agitated by the surroundings and the conversation.

Now to bring out the real guns.

"You should thank my wife, by the way. I didn't want to take your case, didn't want to be drawn into another Hull mess. But Sandra — she's smarter than I am. She saw the value of working for you, and I have to say, she was right."

"I'll send her a card."

"I'm sure she'll cherish it. Now, when I approached this project, I started with the assumption that you were lying about the hacker."

"Mr. Porter —"

"Hold on. You don't want to tell me the truth and that's fine. I'm simply letting you know that I made that assumption in order to proceed with my work. Because I had to ask myself, if the hacker story is a lie, which it is, then this code is no code at all — which is also true. You didn't try hard to hide the meaning behind the letters, and that tells me that you knew all along about Libby Holman. More importantly, you knew she had been cursed."

"Cursed?"

"Don't start insulting me. Back then, no witch so much as whispered about magic without the Hull family knowing. If you didn't know about Libby's curse before this, you certainly figured it out before you brought those initials to my wife. Now, the information you were missing, the thing you really sought in hiring me, was a name. You wanted to know who was responsible for the curse."

"Do you know the answer?"

Picking a piece of cheese from between his teeth, Max said, "I'm guessing that you hope to use this information, and all that goes with it, against Tucker. After all, with the Hulls in control of the use of magic back then, he also would be responsible for its misuse. Of course, it could have been the Magi Group to blame. That's okay, too, as far as you're concerned. Either way, it helps you and hurts one or both of them."

Shaking her head as her eyes rolled upward, she said, "Yes, yes, Mr. Porter. You are very smart and have figured everything out. So, do you have a name or not?"

"Certainly. Marlyn Chester."

Cecily stood and her man came over to hold her chair. She brushed the commonness of the place from her skirt. "Thank you. You can send your bill to my office. Mr. Pescatore will make sure you are promptly paid."

With a slight bow, the pock-marked Mr. Pescatore said, "Yes, ma'am."

Max sipped the last of his soda, making sure it slurped at the bottom. He set it down and feigned concern. "Don't you want to know who she is? What family she comes from? Her history?"

Cecily said, "Oh, my people can find —"

"No, they can't." He spoke harsh enough to freeze her and tense up Mr. Pescatore. "If they could, you would never have hired us. But it's more than that. You are deep into this power struggle and wouldn't be dumb enough to waste resources on finding a name unless it was extremely important."

She whirled back, placing a firm fist on the table as she leaned over him. "Did it ever occur to you, in your entire smug attitude, that I used you? That I sent you on a fool's errand so that my enemies would waste their time following you while I set the stage for my takeover?"

"Yes, actually, it did cross my mind. But then, I went ahead and found Marlyn Chester's family."

She faltered. "What?"

"I found her family. I spoke with her daughter. I told her everything I knew, and you know what she did — ah, I can see on your face you know exactly what she did. That's right. She gave me a very special canister."

Cecily's nostrils flared, and Max worried she might take a swing at him. He didn't want to get in a fistfight with her — especially with her bodyguard so near. She covered up her emotions with her usual stern mask.

"I suppose you have a price in mind," she said.

"I do. See, I'm sick of being caught between all of you. I never wanted any of this crap you all keep slinging around. So, I'm auctioning off the container. Highest price that includes my freedom from all of you wins."

"Tell me when and where, and I'll see that I have the highest bid."

Max stood and put out his hand, but she did not shake it. He mimed tipping a hat, started to leave, and then stopped. "I almost forgot to mention — it addition to finding Marlyn Chester's daughter, I also learned her maiden name. It might interest you. Before she married William Chester, her name was Marlyn Hull. Imagine that. The witch who cursed Libby Holman was a Hull."

Cecily waved off the idea. "She wouldn't be the first Hull to be called a witch."

"True. But she may be the first Hull witch to curse a member of the Reynolds family. I assume they would not be pleased to learn of this."

"Are you trying to blackmail me?"

"I don't do that."

"Then what? You obviously have something in mind to exchange for your silence."

Max hoped he looked calm and casual despite the lie he was about to tell. "Oh, no, I've given you the wrong impression. I've already notified them about your family's treachery."

"You what?"

"I imagine the eldest Reynolds is learning about it all right now. It's all over for you."

Cecily's hands rolled into white-knuckle fists at her sides. Through clamped teeth, she managed, "Why?"

"Because I plan to end up on top of this mess. I'm not your pawn. I refuse to be beholden to you or Tucker or Mother Hope or anybody else." Max turned on his heel and walked away.

He rode the escalator down and headed toward the exit.

When he walked by the restrooms, he darted inside, took the first available stall, and pulled out his cellphone.

"Hey, Ghostman, you ready?"

Max said, "She's all yours, J."

"Don't worry, boss. I'll follow her wherever she goes. I got PB's car this time."

"Good. Get to it."

Chapter 20

AN HOUR LATER, Max went to Maria Cortez-Kane's house to visit with PB. Sandra and Drummond met up with him there, too. It was risky having everyone at Maria's place, but Max wanted to make sure PB was recovering. Plus, he worried about Jammer J, and looking after one Sandwich Boy gave Max the sense that the other would be okay.

Besides, provoking Cecily Hull had pushed the ball over the hill. Now it was rolling, building speed, and nothing could stop it. Max had no choice but to keep going.

After spending a short time watching PB sleep in the guest room, Max went downstairs to the kitchen where Sandra and Maria sipped coffee. He pecked his wife on the cheek before fixing his own mug. Drummond hovered by the door to the garage.

"You feeling any better?" Max asked Maria.

She brushed back her disheveled hair. "Oh, sure. I love having a runaway in my house that's been shot while I watched. Couldn't be happier." She slammed her hand on the table, rattling the silverware, and then stormed out of the room.

In a low voice, Sandra said, "Give her time. She's actually doing okay."

Drummond flew in closer to Max. "She might be fine, but I'm not. What were you thinking going to see Cecily Hull alone?"

"I wasn't alone," Max said. "J was with me. Besides, my bluff worked."

"Yeah, about that — what exactly did you do? I mean, I understand shaking up a suspect and then following them to see what they do, but what's all this with the canister? Aren't we supposed to be looking for Madame Vansandt's eye so she'll help us free Dr. Connor?"

Max took Maria's seat and drank some coffee. "We don't need that eye anymore. Even if we had it, I doubt Madame Vansandt would help us. She's with the Magi Group, after all."

"That was a set up."

"Perhaps. But look how she treated her own student. You really think she's going to play fair with us?"

"You think that canister is any better? Whatever magic is in it came from a witch — a Hull witch, at that."

Max's fingers tapped the side of his coat. "The only thing we can trust hasn't changed — they all hate each other more than they hate us. It doesn't matter, though, because we were never going to get that eye."

"Oh?"

"Cecily Hull already has it."

Maria threw open the door and leveled a burning look on Max. "How do you know that? Did you see it? Can you be sure that it's the real thing?"

Setting his mug down, Max let her questions hang until he saw the manic flare leave her face. "I did not see the eye. I didn't need to. When we spoke, she confirmed everything in the way she behaved, the words she said, and those she didn't. She knew, for example, all about Libby Holman and the curse. She knew that there was a container holding great magic. And she wanted it. She needs it. For the same reason, she took Madame Vansandt's eye — protection. Right now, living in North Carolina, I suspect there are only two living witches old enough and powerful enough to cast these special, ancient spells — Madame Vansandt and Mother Hope."

Sandra clicked her nails against the side of the mug. "Oh, she's clever. She takes the witch's eye as a warning to Mother Hope."

"Partially. But she also has it at her disposal. Most importantly, as long as she has possession of the eye, she doesn't have to worry about others using the eye against her."

Maria scoffed. "That means nothing. You don't have any proof of any of it."

"We have the proof of what has not happened. If Tucker Hull or Mother Hope had possession of your mentor's eye, they would have used it — either against each other or against Cecily."

"Somebody else might have it."

"If that were the case, then Cecily Hull would be frantically searching for it. But she's not. She would have paid me double, maybe even triple, to find that eye. But she's not. Instead, she's searching for Marlyn Chester's canister. Trust me on this. I know when my instincts are shooting true. Cecily Hull has Madame Vansandt's eye."

Maria lifted her head and snarled before walking out of the kitchen. Drummond snickered. "Charming gal."

Max checked his watch — four hours since his meeting with Cecily. To his ghost partner, he said, "Will you do me a favor? Please go check on Jammer J. I don't want him getting into any serious trouble because of us."

"You got it."

Once Drummond disappeared, Sandra took Max's hand and led him back to PB's room. They lingered for a few minutes, watching the boy's chest rise and fall. Then she escorted Max out onto the balcony.

The sky had turned a dark, evening blue. Sandra dropped her head back and closed her eyes. "I can't remember the last case that made me so tired."

"Don't know if we can classify this one as an actual case, but it certainly is exhausting."

Max paused to look at his wife. He stroked her arm. She pressed into his touch.

"I'm worried about you," she said.

"Me?"

"Don't pretend everything is under control. I know you heard Madame Vansandt as well as I did. She said I failed. She said you're still cursed."

Max rubbed his chest. The mark stung at his touch. "I've

been so busy trying to stay ahead of everybody, I haven't really thought about it."

"Well, I have. Maria and I talked about what could be done."

He dropped his hands and his voice. "There's nothing to do. Not yet. You tried, and you brought me back, so you succeeded. It may not have been perfect, but you did fine."

"This is not *fine*. You're not *fine*. That curse is like a ticking time bomb. You really want to ignore it until it's too late?"

"What should I do? Run around, hold my head, and cry?" The air felt colder as the sun went down for the night. "You know we work best when we fight our way through these things. That's what I'm doing. But we can't go worrying about something we have no control over."

"We do have control. I do. That is, I will. Soon."

Max shook his head. "You can't keep digging deeper into witchcraft." But he could see the determination on her face.

She hugged him, laying her head on his chest. "I promise to be careful."

He held her back, his hands on her biceps. "Nothing good is going to come from being a witch."

"That's the point — making it into something good. I mean, why would magic exist if it's only purpose was evil? Life doesn't work like that. Things simply are and it's people that turn it into good or evil. Well, I'm going to learn how to use this stuff and make it good. Healing you, saving you, that's good."

"Excuse me," Drummond said, and Max wondered how much he had overheard. "Sorry to interrupt anything, but J should be pulling up any minute."

"Is he okay?" Max asked.

"Looks fine to me. Although he's driving like a lunatic."

They heard a car screech its tires as it braked hard around front. Max shared one last look with Sandra — a look that promised to keep loving each other no matter how troubling their conversation felt. He hated when they had to share that kind of look.

Downstairs, Jammer J made a ruckus calling out for everybody. In short order, Max and Sandra had met him in the dining room. Maria came a moment later while Drummond circled from above.

Jammer J beamed as he placed his backpack on the fine wood table beneath a tasteful chandelier. "You won't believe what happened to me." With rapid-fire delivery, he told his story.

After getting the call from Max, J sprinted outside the mall. He slowed down, remembering that he was supposed to be hidden, and casually strolled to PB's car. Well, PB's stolen car.

Earlier, he parked as Max had instructed: one row over and five cars up from Cecily Hull's slick Benz — a silver convertible with a black ragtop and a personalized plate reading HULL7. Following her was going to be a snap. Her car stood out like a raging bonfire in the desert at night.

From Winston-Salem, she went south into Lexington, and then burned up Route 64 going east into Asheboro. For over an hour, J followed her. Twice, he thought she might have spotted him, but after a while, he decided she was simply an erratic driver. He wondered if she might be heading to the zoo — it was the only thing he knew in Asheboro — but she took a side road south into Chatham County.

He let a pickup get between them and hung back as much as he dared. The road had become a rural winding mess, walled in with trees and fields. The numerous sharp turns kept her from flooring the Benz, but it also meant she had more opportunities to glance in her rearview mirror — more opportunities to discover J.

Overall, the ride was both exciting and boring — long and drawn out, yet he had to constantly be paying attention to her behavior. Still, he had to admit, he liked the job.

"Anytime you want following done, I'm your man."

Twenty minutes of backroads ended when Cecily pulled into a gas station sitting on the corner of a crossroads. She walked inside, and that's when J decided to take some initiative. He parked on the side of the road, grabbed his backpack, and scurried to the Benz. She had been courteous enough to leave the car unlocked.

He rifled through the glove compartment but found nothing except old receipts and the car's registration. In the armrest, he found twenty dollars and a few old CDs — horrible music taste. Disco.

"And then I looked in the back," he said, his chest filling up. Perched in the middle, he saw a leather bowling ball bag. She would be coming back soon. If he got caught, he'd be screwing everything up for the boss and for PB. So, he unzipped the bag, covered it with his backpack and dumped it over. Then he zipped up the bag and sprinted for his car. He didn't make it in but had to dive behind the side. Peeking over the hood, he watched her get in the Benz, glance back at her bowling bag, buckle up, and drive off.

"I was worried that losing her wouldn't be worth what I did, but then I looked in the backpack. That's when I knew I had to get back here fast as I could."

Max pulled the backpack over. It was heavy. "What is it?"

"Just look."

With a skeptical look, Max opened the backpack. Inside, he saw a skull. A skull with an iron gag latched around it.

"Holy shit," Max said.

J grinned. "I know."

Drummond peeked from above. "Is that?"

"I think so," Max said, tilting the bag so Sandra could see.

She nodded. "That's got to be Dr. Connor."

Max closed the backpack. His mind swarmed with thoughts of the Magi Group, the Hulls, the war between them, Madam Vansandt, Libby Holman, and Dr. Connor. The connections formed fast. He could almost see lightning strike between his thoughts.

"We've got to hurry," he said. "Cecily Hull thinks she still has Dr. Connor's skull. And she has Madame Vansandt's eye."

Drummond snapped his fingers. "She's making her move. With you holding the canister, she's thinking she's got to try now or she might lose."

"But she already lost," J said. "I got that skull from her."

Sandra pointed at Max, and he could tell that she had started putting it together, too. "She doesn't know it yet. Neither does anybody else."

"Exactly," Max said. "You know just like they've been watching us, they've been watching each other, too."

Drummond pursed his lips. "Which means that they're all figuring this out right now. They all know she's trying to make a big move."

"And they're all going to follow her to the same place," Sandra added.

J laughed. "I'd love to see their faces when she opens that bag and it's empty."

Max glanced around the room. He didn't like where his mind had taken him, but his gut said this would be the best play.

Sandra must have read his face because she placed a hand on her hip and shook her head. "No. You are not going there."

"If we're going to stop this, if we're going to be free of this insanity that we've been stuck inside for the last bunch of years, this is our chance. They'll all be in the same place. And we have the skull. The power is on our side."

Drummond nodded. "He's right, doll. Don't worry, though. I'll keep him safe."

"Then I'm coming, too," she said.

Max shouldered the backpack. "You can't."

"I'm not giving you a choice."

The firmness in her eyes told him that arguing would be futile. "Fine."

"Are you nuts?" Drummond said. "They can threaten her. Force you to do whatever they want."

Sandra glared at them. "Have you two boys forgotten everything I've done for us?"

Not wanting to prolong a settled discussion, Max pulled up his maps app and handed it to J. "Show me where you got the skull. Assuming Cecily planned to cast a spell with the eye and this skull, I imagine it would be most effective near midnight.

Right?"

"Yeah," Sandra said. "Especially because the kind of spell needing those objects would be one of those dark, ancient kinds. From what I've learned, the witching hour is called that for a reason."

"So we've got a few hours to figure out where she went, come up with a plan of action, and get ourselves there."

Maria spoke causing everyone to jump. "I know where she's going."

"How long have you been there?"

She entered the dining room and glanced at the phone. "Oh, I know exactly where she's going. You remember what Madame Vansandt said? That the ancient spells and curses of this nature needed a location of strong negative energy. Well, there's one place out there — a terrible place that flows with nothing but negative energy."

"Then that has to be where she's going. What's the place?"

Maria scanned the room, making sure everybody paid attention. Her face had hardened into that of a calculating mind. *A witch*, Max thought. When she spoke, he knew it to be true.

"She's going to the Devil's Tramping Ground."

Chapter 21

THEY DROVE IN SILENCE. Max and Sandra stewed in their thoughts, each shifting and sighing and staring while the streetlights rolled across their faces. He parked in their driveway and took a moment to look at his house. It had been days since either of them had seen their home. All brick, large lawn, and a hefty price tag — more home than they ever thought they'd own.

"You sure it's okay to be here?" Sandra asked.

"Not sure of anything. But I think there's no point in hiding anymore. Everybody is either at this Devil's Tramping Ground or on their way. Drummond will watch over that area for us. He'll warn us if anything happens. But really, they're going to have to wait for us — we've got Dr. Connor's skull."

"They don't know that."

"Not yet. But they will. Sooner or later."

Entering the house, Max marveled at how it smelled new. A few days without anybody inside and it had taken on that stale yet oddly fresh new aroma of an empty house. Sandra clumped upstairs to take a shower while Max went to his study. As tired as he felt, he still found the energy to giggle at the idea of having a study.

He eased behind his desk and rubbed his face. The situation had moved faster than he had expected, and he wondered if he had any real control. Sending Jammer J off on a crucial mission with a vital message meant trusting the outcome to the skills of a teenager. He had done it before but not with so much in the balance. At least he knew Maria would look after PB. If it all fell apart, if Max and Sandra never came back, at least that much good would come out of it. PB would be fine.

He pulled a blank piece of paper from a drawer and an expensive pen as well. Unscrewing the cap, he looked at the empty page like a daunting mountain daring him to take the first step. He thought about what he would write as he hovered the pen over the paper.

After a minute, he set the pen down and picked up the phone. On the second ring, his mother answered. "Hi, Mom."

"Maxwell, I'm so happy you called."

They chatted about nothing important for a little. He asked how she was doing, and she blabbed on for five minutes about her adventures with doctors and health insurance. While she spoke, he picked up the pen again and figured he knew enough to write the title — *Last Will and Testament of Maxwell Samuel Porter*.

"Enough about me," his mother said, her voice bubbling with excitement. He understood — though they spoke every week, he rarely was the one to reach out. "Tell me how you are. I take it you've got some good news?"

I, Maxwell Samuel Porter, being of sound mind ... "Sorry, Mom. I know you're hoping I'm calling about a baby, but she's not pregnant."

"Oh. Well, is everything okay? You sound a bit strange."

"I'm okay. Very tired."

"You work too hard. Whenever I call, you're doing research for one client or another. You've got to take time for yourself. Go on a vacation. Or at least take your wife on a date. How can I expect any grandchildren, if you're exhausted all the time?"

To my wife, I leave ... "A vacation sounds nice right now. Maybe when I'm done with my current assignment."

"That'd be smart. You listen to your mother. I know a thing or two."

"I know."

"Don't give me that 'I know' business. You need to listen to me. I've been looking out for you and your health my whole life. That's my job. So, let me do my job."

To the boys I know as PB and Jammer J ... "That's true. You have been looking out for me. Makes me think of when I was a kid and I thought the jackets in my closet turned into monsters at night."

His mother rumbled a soft chuckle. "You had quite an imagination. The teeth on the zippers became big mouths that wanted to gobble you up. For two nights, you refused to sleep in your room."

"But you fought them for me."

"I tried. I did that thing they tell parents where I filled a spray bottle with water and told you it was monster spray. But you were too smart for that."

Under the authority of Sandra Porter, I wish to set up the Marshall Drummond College Scholarship ... "I don't know why I did that. If I believed the coats could become monsters, why couldn't I accept your monster spray?"

"It sounded phony. Because you remember what actually worked, don't you? The truth. I simply told you that monsters didn't exist. We sat in your room and waited until night, and then I turned out the lights. I took you by the hand, and we opened the closet door and touched the coats. After that, you had no problems because you knew there were no monsters."

Max dropped the pen. "I wish that were still true. But I know better now. There are monsters. Real ones."

His mother lost all the forced frivolity she usually employed. It was scary hearing her speak serious. "Yes, there are. People can be evil things."

"Was my father? We never talk much about him."

"At times. At times, he was wonderful. I guess that's the way most people are." Like turning a light switch, his mother shifted back to her normal self. "Why are you asking such things? What good comes from dwelling on the bad stuff in life?"

"Sorry. It was just on my mind. I've got to get going. I have an important meeting tonight. But I wanted to call and, oh, I don't know. I hope I've done good by you, made you feel that you did a good job raising me."

"Of course, I do. I'm proud of you all the time. I love you."

Max smiled. "I love you, too, Mom. Good-bye."

As he hung up the phone, Sandra walked in. Her hair was wet and she wore clean clothes. The delightful aroma of shampoo and soap covered her skin. She placed a fresh pair of jeans, clean boxers, and a clean shirt on the back of a chair. "You about ready?"

"I'll put those on and we can go."

"You hungry? Want me to make a sandwich or anything for the drive?"

"Sure. That'd be great."

After she left, Max picked up his pen and read over the paper. Satisfied, he signed it at the bottom and quickly got dressed.

Chapter 22

SANDRA TOOK THE WHEEL and guided them all the way out to Route 64. On his phone, Max juggled between his maps app to help Sandra and his browser to research the Devil's Tramping Ground.

"There isn't much solid info here," he grumbled. "Mostly just legends."

"That's better than nothing."

So, Max told her the legends. From what he could find, the Devil's Tramping Ground had existed since the birth of Chatham County. On the surface, it didn't seem that strange — a circle of tramped down grass about forty feet in diameter sitting in the woods. Except according to the locals of the time, nothing would grow there. If they left a bottle or a hat or any object in the circle, they would return the next day to find that the object had been violently thrown aside. Supposedly, anybody who dared attempt to spend the night in the circle ran off a raving madman.

Nobody knows what was really wrong with the place, but there were plenty of hypotheses. The most prominent, and the one that gave the ground its name, was that the Devil himself rose at night and paced the circle while laying plans for the suffering and destruction of mankind. However, another story traced back to before the European settlers arrived.

According to that tale, two native tribes had clashed in a massive battle that converged on the area. Casualties were high, and the blood of both tribes seeped into the ground, killing the soil and preventing life from taking root. One tribe was decimated to extinction. The other tribe, horrified by their deeds, left the area forever. They relocated eastward on the coast, forming the Croatan tribe which connected with another great mystery — the lost colony of Roanoke Island.

"Those are both good stories," Sandra said.

"Not much in the way of facts, though."

"It still confirms what Maria said — that the area is filled with significant negative energy. Perfect for the kinds of spells and curses we've been dealing with. I imagine covens have been using the circle for the last hundred years or more."

"It appears teens use it now as a party spot."

"That figures."

After leaving the highway, they wound through one twisted road after another until they reached the intersection of Siler City Glendon Road and Route 902. On the map the place was labeled Harper's Crossroads. Odd enough that an intersection in the middle of nowhere had a name that showed up on a map, but supposedly the Devil's Tramping Ground Road connected due north — except when Sandra turned north on Siler City Glendon Road, all they saw surrounding them was a large field with head-high grass.

Unless ... Max pointed to what looked like the narrow driveway that led through the fields to a farmhouse. No road sign. No indication that a road even existed.

Sandra pulled a sharp turn. The GPS in Max's phone said they were on the correct road.

"Guess the locals or maybe even the county took down the road sign to keep the tourists of the weird away," Max said.

The area they drove through struck Max with its serenity. Beautiful trees in a thick forest on the left side. On the right, endless fields. About a mile up on the left, Max noticed a little cutaway with a few cars parked. It stood out because there was nothing around to stop for — no homes or businesses or anything. Just field and forest.

They kept driving on, but after another mile the forest gave way to a typical suburban development. Max didn't have to say a word. Sandra took the first opportunity to U-turn and head back.

She parked the car near the others, and the instant they stepped out, Max knew they were in the right place. The air smelled dead. The temperature chilled his skin. Lime-green fungus dotted the trees. He could feel the threat pressing in from the soaked bark as if the forest had been mutated into a shallow bog.

Shouldering the backpack, Max led the way with a flashlight. He didn't have to go far. Gnarled tree roots formed natural stairs leading up into the wooded area, and only twenty or so feet in, he saw it — the wide, blackened circle littered with beer cans, bottles, and cardboard boxes. Apparently, the Devil got tired of removing the trash from teen parties.

Though close to the road, the circle felt secluded, protected, hidden in the darkness of the trees. A mound of earth held the center of the circle with the remnants of fires set for warmth or possibly offerings. Several trails led off deeper into the woods.

Max would have loved to explore the whole area, but unfortunately, they were not alone. Mother Hope and Leon Moore stood in front of the north trail with a burning torch stuck in the ground. Opposite Max and Sandra, on the west side, Tucker Hull and the Pale Man stood with their torch. And to the south stood Cecily Hull and her bodyguard, Mr. Pescatore. Flicking off the flashlight, Max waited for his eyes to adjust to the amber torches.

Nobody moved, but everybody watched. Eyes darted from face to face. Fingers twitched. Tongues licked dry lips.

Max noticed that Cecily held the bowling bag at her side. She had to know it was empty. The weight of the skull and the iron gag dug the backpack into Max's shoulder, and that bowling bag had to be light. A bluff that appeared to be holding the others back — good for her. But that bluff would only last so long, and since Max held the real threat, he could stop her anytime he wanted. The way her eyes fixated on his backpack told him she shared the same thoughts.

Tucker stood with his legs apart and his eyes squinting like a cowboy in an old western. Since his resurrection, he had been burning through bodies. His current choice — a square-jawed, military man — appeared to be holding up better than the others Max had seen. But it wasn't enough to convince Max of Tucker's strength.

Not that the patriarch of the Hull family was weak — after all, Max had been there when Tucker fought a hellish spirit in the depths beneath Baxter House. But that had been over a year ago, and other than that moment, Tucker had displayed little in the way of power. Perhaps returning from the grave had cost him more than he cared to admit. That had certainly been the prevailing hypothesis to explain why Hull had failed to take out Max and his wife.

The only problem with that line of thinking was Mother Hope. Max watched the old woman closely. She snatched glances at Tucker but refused to look too long. She was afraid of him. That was enough to give Max a shiver.

Leon, the Pale Man, and Mr. Pescatore all watched each other like growling dogs aching to be let off the leash. Drummond slipped out of the woods and weaved around the groups, observing up close the things Max inferred from a distance.

Max saw that Drummond had no trouble moving close to Mother Hope. The energy of the Devil's Tramping Ground must have prevented Mother Hope's wards from working. *That's why she's scared.* Not simply because of her vulnerability to Drummond, but her vulnerability to Tucker as well. He existed in both the living and the dead worlds. Her wards must have protected her ever since his return. But not here.

Tucker lifted a hand. He spoke with a thick, wet voice. "We all know why we came. We all know what's at stake. But unless my dear Cecily can produce the skull, there is no point in letting this situation escalate."

"Yes," Mother Hope said, shifting on her feet like an anxious child. "Show us."

Displaying nothing but calm confidence, Cecily glanced at her watch. "The witching hour isn't here yet. You'll have to wait."

Tucker bent down and picked up two rocks from the

blackened earth. One, he threw into the woods. They all listened to it clatter against the trees and thud into the ground. The other rock he tossed at Max's feet. "How about you? You're the one who trades in knowledge. Does she have the skull?"

"She always had the skull," Max said. "That's why nobody could find it. I suspect the day she took it was the day she committed to overthrowing you."

"But what about now? Does she have the skull now?"

Cecily's focus on Max was palpable — a bitter blend of dare and threat. He could feel the truth rising in his throat, but he swallowed it down. He had no idea when he should reveal that he held the skull, but his instincts told him to hold back. Besides, if at that moment, he revealed that he had the skull, all the pressure would leave Cecily and fall upon him.

"Well, you clearly don't have it," Max said and felt a tinge of satisfaction watching Tucker bristle. "Mother Hope also doesn't have the skull. If she did, she would have used it to destroy you the first chance she got — which would have been long before tonight. So, I guess we'll have to wait until the witching hour to find out."

"Perhaps," Tucker said, miming the weighing of possibilities in his hands. "Perhaps not."

The Pale Man raised his handgun which set off a chain reaction of appearing weapons. Leon whipped out a long-barreled revolver while Mr. Pescatore had a straight-forward semi-automatic. Safeties were clicked off, hammers were cocked, bullets were chambered.

Drummond floated into the middle of the circle. "Max, pal, don't let this fall apart. We're not that kind of people."

But Max found the idea that they might all shoot each other appealing. Still, he knew Drummond was right, and he had no intention of risking Sandra's life just to see his enemies destroy themselves. "Everybody calm down. No need for all the guns."

Looking younger and stronger than ever before, Leon said, "Sorry, Max, but some people only respond to a little violence."

"Not these people. Maybe you guys with guns want to shoot

holes into each other, but you all know the families you're working for. You really think a bullet is going to do any good against Tucker Hull?"

"It'll do damage. And it'll certainly do damage to little Cecily."

Cecily glowered at Leon but said nothing. The three men with guns continued to point them at each other while their bosses stood still and watched.

"Come on," Max said. "You can't be serious. Are you really willing to kill yourself for these people?"

The muzzle of the Pale Man's gun had a slight tremor. Of course. He was a hired gun and nothing more. He'd kill for money, but he'd never sacrifice himself for a client. Leon, on the other hand, was a zealot. Anything Mother Hope asked of him, he'd do. Simple. As for Cecily's man, Max had a big question mark.

Mother Hope entered the fray with a simplicity of her own. "Cecily, I know you want to take control of the Hull family. Well, I'm agreeable to that. My Magi exist to maintain order in this world. We've let the Hull family operate for decades because order existed. Only now have things become unacceptable."

Tucker clasped his hands behind his back. "If you're going to try to sway my own family against me, you shouldn't start with lies. The truth, Cecily, is that Mother Hope is striking not for order but for domination. She figures, since you've yet to defeat me, that if you join her, she can easily control you."

"Lies! If I wanted to destroy your family, I would have done it before they resurrected you. There have been plenty of weak fools running the Hulls since you died." To Cecily, she added, "You know I'm right. You would have taken over earlier but you were still a child. Join me against Tucker and we can win this. I'm the only one here who can make that happen with you. I can see to it that you get what you long for. But in order to do that, I need Dr. Connor's skull."

"Don't be an idiot," Tucker said. "If you listen to that foolishness, then nobody will win."

"That skull is all that stands between you and immense power."

"She's a witch. You've been around their kind long enough to know that you can't trust a witch."

Cecily raised the bowling bag. "You want this? Both of you?" She cheated her head to the side, enough to see her bodyguard. "You can have it."

"Shit," Max whispered. He put his hand on Sandra's shoulder. "Get ready to duck."

With an unpleasant grunt, Cecily hurled the bag high into the center of the circle. As Tucker and Mother Hope looked up at the bag, Mr. Pescatore opened fire.

Tucker's shoulder popped back, and the world became a torrent of explosive noise and staggered flashes of light. Max shoved Sandra. "Go!" They dropped to the dirt and crawled behind a large tree.

Peeking around the trunk, Max saw that everyone had found cover behind trees standing or fallen. Shots spit bark into the air. Cecily's man reloaded his weapon before spraying bullets near Mother Hope. Leon repositioned and fired back. But doing so left him open on the other side, and the Pale Man caught Leon in the leg.

"Get down!" Sandra grabbed Max's jacket and wrenched him back behind the tree. "You'll get yourself shot."

"We've got to see what's happening."

"They're killing each other. That's what's happening. As long as they don't see us, they won't remember we're here because we're not shooting anybody."

More shots blared away. Max and Sandra scrunched lower to the ground, holding each other tight. His face pressed into the top of her head, and even the delightful smell of her hair would not comfort him. This was only three men with guns — he couldn't imagine what a war between armies would feel like.

Drummond came over, his face lit up like a giddy boy watching a schoolyard fight. "Wow, they're really going at it."

"Can't you do anything?" Max said. "Eventually, they'll be done with each other and then we're screwed."

"Well, don't try to run for it. You'll get shot."

"Stating the obvious isn't helpful."

"Maybe next time you'll be smart and bring a gun along. Don't you know anything yet? You always bring a gun to a gunfight."

"Really? You're going to go with a version of *I told you so?* Well, I'm sorry that I'm still not all that good with a gun. I don't usually need one. I've usually got something I can ..." Max's eyes darted around as he thought over the idea in his head.

Drummond floated down to the ground. "I don't like that look. What are you thinking?"

"I don't have a gun, but I've got a skull."

Sandra raised her head and joined Drummond's concern. "Please, honey, don't do this."

"If we stay here, we'll eventually get shot."

"But that skull is —"

"It's our chance. Unless one of you has a better idea."

Sandra and Drummond said nothing.

Biting his bottom lip, Max unzipped the backpack and pulled out Dr. Connor's skull. The rusty iron gag made it more hideous and far heavier in his hands. Max arched his head back and inhaled sharply. "Here I go."

Chapter 23

AT THE AGE OF SEVEN, Max attended the wedding of his Aunt Mary to his Uncle Claude. Aunt Mary thought it a wonderful idea (and oh how cute!) to have Max walk the rings down the aisle. On the day of the wedding, Max's mother handed him a satin pillow with two gold bands tied to the pillow with lace. She pushed him into a line of well-dressed adults waiting outside the church doors and said, "All you've got to do is walk to the end and hand the pillow to your grandpa."

"Okay, Mommy," he said, clueless as to what this was all about.

"Whatever you do, don't drop the pillow."

Music started playing inside the church and the line slowly moved. As he stepped closer to the doors, his cheap suit grew itchier and the satin pillow grew heavier. Suddenly, all the water he had drunk that morning pressed against the walls of his bladder.

At the doors, a lady Max had never met put out her hand for him to stop. She had a clipboard in her other hand and counted aloud, "And 5, and 4, and 3, and 2, and 1." She opened the door and motioned with her head for Max to enter.

Walking down that aisle, that little boy felt that the fate of his world depended on his ability to keep that pillow from falling while not peeing his pants in front of a crowd. Max never imagined he would feel that pressure again. He was wrong.

Holding the gagged-skull of Dr. Connor over his head, Max stepped carefully into the circle. His bladder threatened to let loose while his mind tried to maintain focus on not dropping the skull. From the corner of his eye, he saw the Pale Man aiming a weapon, but Tucker shoved the man aside.

Max looked across at Mr. Pescatore. As he raised his handgun toward Max, Drummond soared across the Tramping Ground and threw his fist into the man's head. Both the man and the ghost cried out, but only the man fell to the ground unconscious.

That left Leon, but Max had no worries there. Leon understood the world of magic. Where the other two were essentially henchmen, Leon provided more than mere muscle to Mother Hope.

Once in the center of the circle, Max lowered his arm. "This fighting, all of it, has got to stop. It hasn't always been this way. I know better than all of you. I've researched the Hull family extensively. I know your history better than any other. Even you, Tucker. And Mother Hope, your Magi Group has a long history, as well. I've been the one who has researched it from its formation to the present day."

Mother Hope pouted. "Then you know we've always been fighting each other."

"But not always like this. Not to the point of causing this much chaos. You've all become too comfortable with your power. It's corrupted you." Max turned to face Cecily. "All of you."

"I don't have any power," she said.

"Of course you do. You were born into it. Here's the thing about power and corruption. The public don't mind it. That's why you've been able to act as you have all these years. Most of the public don't even know or pay attention, but those that do, they accept a little corruption. They may even expect it. Just like organized crime or politicians, we don't condemn you for exercising your power even if it's blatantly corrupt. Provided you don't mess with our lives. But when you get so comfortable with using your power, when you get greedy to a point that shoves the inequity in our faces, then the public gets upset. That's when criminals go to jail and governments are toppled."

Max walked a gentle arc so he could look into the eyes of each party. Last, he set eyes on his wife. Her confident nod warmed his heart. Of course, he also noticed her hands locked together in a white-knuckle clench, but the fact that she still found the strength to urge him on was enough.

"Ever since we moved down here and learned of the world you all live in, we've been content to let you have it. Manipulate the city and the state with magic and money, and we wouldn't bother you at all. We simply wanted to live our lives in peace. But you wouldn't have it. Your corruption, your greed, spilled over until you impacted our lives more and more. Well, as the representative of the public in this case, I'm here to tell you that we've had it. We're sick of cringing and cowering every time we hear the name Hull. We're sick of dodging and weaving the gauntlet of spells that the Magi and the Hulls throw out onto the world. It all stops now."

Mother Hope spit on the ground. "It only stops when the Hulls stop using magic."

"Why?" Tucker said. "So you and all the witches can do as you please?"

Max raised his voice above the bickering. "You have a chance right now. All of you can walk away from this. Tucker will return to the dead where he belongs, and he'll give control of the family to Cecily. Cecily will end all affairs dealing with magic and focus on legitimate businesses for the Hulls. Mother Hope will disband the Magi Group. That's it. You either fix this now or I will set Dr. Connor free, and you can all try to control her in a game of magic Russian roulette."

"Nice speech," Tucker said. "Except your threat is empty. Unless you brought a hacksaw, you can't break through that witch's gag. It may be rusty, but it's still iron."

Max searched the faces surrounding him. "Is that what you all answer? You want to see if I'm bluffing?"

With hesitation, Cecily managed to take a single step forward. "Tucker's right. The gag is solid all around. You can't cut her loose. You try to pick the lock and we'll take you down before you can even start."

"Mother Hope? Are you like the rest — too greedy for power?"

The old woman shrugged. "These two already refused your offer. What does it matter what I think?"

"I'm sorry to hear that. Whatever happens, you all had a chance."

Tucker sneered. "Enough already. Whoever kills him first will get Dr. Connor."

Max did not wait for the guns to rise. He brought his hand down fast, smashing the skull on the hard mound in the center of the Devil's circle. The old bones shattered like brittle pottery, and Max had one unique second in which he saw markings on the inside of the gag. Then Dr. Connor's curse ripped to shreds.

An explosive force lifted Max off the ground. Heat and sulphuric odors pressed him higher into the air and cast him to the edge of the circle. Like a sharp knife cutting the skin, Max felt the mark on his chest slice open. He cried out and clutched the wound.

While his heart hammered against his chest, he forced himself up. Everybody lay on the ground from the explosion. He looked back for Sandra. Coughing, she waved him on.

He rolled to his knees, took a few breaths, and put one foot firmly onto the ground. Groaning, he pushed up until he could slip his other foot underneath. Though still crouched over, at least he was standing.

Before he could look into the circle, the light scent of rosemary perfume drifted toward him. The perspiration dotting his skin beaded and froze. Max lifted his head.

A young, attractive woman stood before him. No, she didn't stand. She floated a few inches above the ground.

Dr. Ashley Connor.

She placed a slender finger against her cheek. "Well, well. Max Porter. Why, just the man I've been dying to kill."

Chapter 24

MAX COULD NOT MOVE. Not because of some spell or magical force, but because of fear. True terror. His muscles would not react to the will of his brain. All he could see was Dr. Connor gliding towards him. All he could hear was the rapid pounding of his heart.

Five feet away from him, she stopped and spun like a ballerina. "Death looks good on me, don't you think? I don't think I looked this beautiful in years. In fact, I think I started to lose my beauty the day you walked into my office."

Max tried to swallow but his throat constricted against it.

"That's it? You're going to stand there and say nothing?" In a flash, she had her face right in front to him. Her anger heated his skin as if he sat too close to a campfire. "Oh, don't worry. I remember exactly how to get a rise out of you." She turned her attention to those behind him. "All I have to do is play with your sweetheart. What's her name? Sally? Sandy?"

"Sandra," Max growled and found the strength to straighten.

"See that? I knew I could get you moving. But you're still so slow. Allow me to help." She backhanded him like a princess discarding an unwanted servant. When her hand struck, however, it was with a force that no fairy tale princess ever possessed.

Max shot back through the air and slammed into the trees. He thumped into the ground, and his vision blurred as tears filled his eyes. Rolling onto his back, he inhaled and his lungs burned — *I better not have broken another rib.*

Sandra appeared at his side and reached under him. With her help, he managed to get back to his feet.

Mother Hope had moved in towards Dr. Connor. The old woman approached with her head down and her eyes averted. In her hand, Max saw a blue amulet. "Dr. Connor, please."

Dr. Connor reared back but then laughed. "Oh, you've got a little charm to help you see me. Can you hear me, too?"

"Yes. Please, listen. You must be careful. When a witch dies, she has access to great power, but you well know that all power has a cost."

"You want to school me on witchcraft? My family has been dealing in spells since before you were a thought."

"Then I shouldn't have to remind you that the energy you use to appear young or to throw us in the air burns up your time as a ghost. If you don't ration your use of this power, you'll burn up. At best, you'll be reduced to a mound of glowing ash. More likely, you'll end up a soul with no manifestation other than a formless glob."

Dr. Connor tossed her hair back. "But I like looking the way I do. You have no idea what it's like on this side of life."

"But I do know what happens if —"

"You think I'll end up like that bastard, Leed?" She swiped her hand, and like a child plucking a candy, she pulled out a glowing bit of light from the air. "What this mouse thought it could do spying on a lioness like me, I'll never know. Then again, I'll never care."

"Leed!" Drummond said and rushed forward. Tucker leaped out, too, but not toward Dr. Connor. Instead, he tackled Drummond, sending the ghost into the ground.

Max glanced at his chest — the curse. Originally, it had put him in a near-death state. The way it now cut through his skin gave Max a thought. Tucker lived in both the living and dead worlds which was why he could touch Drummond. Since Max could see Leed, then perhaps he, too, had a foot in both worlds.

"Leed?" he said, his voice quivering.

Dr. Connor spun back toward Max. "Oh, you can see your old friend, can you? Well, that does make this a far more satisfying experience." She closed her fingers around Leed and squeezed.

"No!" Drummond yelled but Tucker had him pinned to the ground.

An audible pop halted all who could see Leed. Silver liquid dribbled between Dr. Connor's pale fingers. Drummond uttered a single cry. Thrusting his elbow while twisting his ghostly body, he broke free from Tucker. Instead of attacking Dr. Connor, however, Drummond launched right back into Tucker.

Screaming garbled words, he threw a barrage of punches, knocking Tucker back into the woods. The Pale Man, unable to see the ghosts, watched in disbelief as Tucker gyrated himself until blood splashed from his nose.

Dr. Connor shook her hand, spraying the liquid that had been Leed onto the ground. Grinding his teeth, Max glowered at the witch. He could hear Sandra moving closer to him, and he motioned her back.

"Don't want the wife to play?" Dr. Connor said. "But she's just as much to blame as you."

Tucker kicked Drummond off of him and rose to his feet.

"First," Dr. Connor said, "you and your wife destroyed my office. Then you destroyed my reputation. After all the work disappeared, you turned me into an alcoholic. You made the Hull family lose faith in my abilities."

Tucker moved with surprising grace and speed. He ducked Drummond's wild punch and smashed his fist into the ghost's chin. Dazed, Drummond slipped through several trees as Tucker followed him with another fist ready to strike.

Dr. Connor's eyes flickered like firelight. "It took me some time to return to a position I deserved. But you were there to screw it up again. From the day you arrived in North Carolina, you have hounded me, plagued me, but tonight we see that you cannot destroy me. In fact, I'm stronger than ever."

She thrust out her arm, and Max felt something grab hold of his chest. *The curse!* She raced forward and the unseen pressure on his chest shoved him back until he slammed into a tree.

"Leave him alone!" Sandra charged Dr. Connor, but the

witch merely put out her free hand. Sandra smacked into something hard and fell back.

"What's the matter, little girl? You think the living are the only ones who can create a ward? And here, the Devil's Tramping Ground, well, surely you didn't think you were immune to its effects."

"But the wards against ghosts —"

"It's the other way around here."

Sandra crawled up to the invisible wall that blocked her from getting any further and watched. Max felt the tears falling from his face. Once more, his body had frozen — only this time, it was due to Dr. Connor and not his fear.

Dr. Connor lowered her head and mumbled a few phrases. Though Max could not decipher the words, he knew he wouldn't like the result.

The pain started at once, burning from the mark on his chest even as cold crept up his legs. The heat formed a jagged line down to his stomach. He heard shrieking and looked to Sandra. Only when he saw that she wasn't making the noise did he understand that he was the one crying out.

"Stop it," Mother Hope said. "You don't have much time. If you keep using up the magic you have, we'll never be able to fight Tucker."

Dr. Connor paused to address Mother Hope, and Max slumped forward, heavily panting, grateful for the reprieve. "What are you chattering about?"

"The spell. I need you, a powerful witch that has died — I need you to cast a spell with me so that we may stop Tucker Hull. Cecily has a witch's eye."

"Really? Who?"

"Madame Vansandt."

"That shriveled bitch?"

"With that eye, we can do this. But we must do it now, while the Porter's ghost is keeping Tucker busy."

Dr. Connor's skin reddened as if a fire burned beneath the surface, and she leaned toward Mother Hope. Cackling a laugh, she said, "Why would I ever want to defeat Tucker Hull? I am loyal to the Hulls like my mother was loyal to the Hulls and my grandmother was loyal to the Hulls and even my great-grandmother, too. My family's long line of witches has proudly served the Hulls. Why would I defile that?"

"But —"

Tucker threw Drummond across the circle. The ghost passed through Mother Hope, bringing the old woman to her knees. Her teeth chattered and she hugged her arms tight against the sudden cold.

To Tucker, Dr. Connor said, "If you're done playing with that ghost, we can cast our spell."

With a guilty grin, he wiped his hands on his pants and returned to the circle. Max saw a flash of the charm this man had once possessed, the charm that gave him such control over others, the charm that would help him smile his way forward while destroying those who blocked his path. He strolled by Dr. Connor and put his hand out towards Cecily.

"My dear child, we have been foolish. I have held too strongly to the way the world had been while I was alive. Hundreds of years have fallen away, and the rules I once knew have changed. I now see that the place of a woman has changed as well. Max here, our friend and constant thorn, spoke of seeking peace and stability and avoiding corruption, and I could not agree more. What better way for us to achieve such lofty goals than together?"

"Excuse me?" Cecily inched closer even as her head pulled back.

"Come. You have Madame Vansandt's eye, and I have Dr. Connor. Together, we can destroy the Magi Group and run the Hull family into a prosperous future."

"Together? After I give you the eye, what happens to me?"

"What do you want?"

"You know the answer."

"Yes, I do. Okay. Help me, and you will have proven your worth. We will share the running of the family. You will be president of our business operations, and I shall handle familial and magical concerns. Is that agreeable?"

The triumph that overcame Cecily's face sickened Max. She took Tucker's hand and let him escort her into the circle. "I think we're going to build a happy family."

Tucker stopped Cecily a few feet away, pointing out where Dr. Connor stood so that Cecily did not accidentally walk through the ghost. Then he let go of her hand and put his out, palm up. "The eye?"

From her pocket, Cecily pulled out a small container and handed it over. Tucker nodded to Dr. Connor before facing Max.

"Now, it's over. You and your wife have put up a noble fight. You thwarted a few of the family heads, and you caused a lot of disruption. But you've reached your end."

Max searched for something or someone to help him. But Drummond and Sandra were both injured. Mother Hope looked shaken and unsteady. Leon and the other guns were useless.

Dr. Connor snuggled next to Tucker, kissing his cheek and purring. "Don't worry, Max. I'm going to make sure you live a long, painful life. What I've got in mind will make the curse of Marshall Drummond look like a party trick."

Max felt the weight of the canister in his coat. His shaking fingers lingered over his pocket, but he held back. If he tried to pull out the canister and release it, they would attack him long before he could get the top off. He needed to find an opening.

"No matter what she does to you," Tucker went on, "I can guarantee this much — you will live to see all that you care about razed to the ground. You will watch the Hull family grow stronger and more powerful. Maybe Cecily will become a Senator, and we'll take over the entire state. After that, the country will be easy enough."

Max rolled his eyes. "Why not throw in world domination while you're at it?"

"In time. Perhaps. But there's no need to be greedy."

A painful bubbling erupted in Max's stomach. In the past, when things looked down, he always found a way out. His researcher's mind always managed to uncover an answer. But this time, everywhere he looked he saw failure. The people had all been beaten. The dead could not help. The spells were poised against him.

If only he hadn't smashed Dr. Connor's skull. Perhaps things would have still gone bad, but at least he wouldn't have given Tucker what the man needed. Max had hoped lifting Dr. Connor's curse would have endeared her to him — or at least enticed her to help him against a common enemy — but he should have counted on her loyalty to the Hulls. It was a foolish error, and now it would cost him his life and the life of his love. All because he broke an ancient curse.

Wait. Max's synapses fired off like the finale of a July Fourth fireworks celebration.

Dr. Connor cocked her head to the side. "Max? Are you in there? I fear we may have scared him to the point of insanity."

With a loud snort, Max burst into laughter. He stumbled back, and as his laughter continued, he discovered the will to move returning to his limbs.

Scowling, Dr. Connor said, "Stop that. What's so funny?"

"You. Don't you even want to know who cursed you?"

"I already know. You did."

Dabbing at his eyes while giggling more, Max managed to say, "Not likely. I don't know any serious spells of that caliber. And my wife has only learned the basics. Saving me was luck and some raw talent, but neither of us even knew about an iron gag curse."

"Then who did this to me?" Her skin pulsed dark red.

"Who do you think? Tucker Hull, of course."

Chapter 25

MAX WATCHED DR. CONNOR'S FACE tighten as she narrowed her eyes upon Tucker. A truck rumbled along the road. A dog barked in the distance. The witch shook her head.

"I don't believe it," she said.

"It doesn't matter what you believe," Max said. "It's the truth. Tucker Hull cursed you with that iron gag."

Tucker snickered. "Thank you, Max. Your desperateness only lets my dear witch and I know how close we are to beating you."

"Dr. Connor, look at me. Do I seem desperate to you?" Max waited for her to face him, a glimmer of uncertainty crossing her features. "Think about this and tell me which makes more sense — a man who until a few years ago didn't even know ghosts existed, somehow learned an ancient spell, harnessed the power to cast it, and in doing so, took down the most powerful witch in all of the South, or that Tucker Hull did this to you? After you died, who had access to your corpse? It had to be somebody who knows where you're buried. That's not me. How did Cecily Hull get ahold of your skull, if not stealing it from Tucker? And who among us here has the true know-how to pull off this kind of curse?"

Dr. Connor's skin pulsed as her lips rose in an ugly snarl. "You are a deceiver. You want to turn me against Tucker. But I know all the wrong you've done to me, to us. I'll see you suffer for it."

She charged forward, her hands out like claws, her eyes open wide like her mouth. Max dove to the ground, feeling the cold of the dead rush over him. He rolled to his back.

As she whirled around for another run, he yelled, "Check the gag. Look at the inside."

"You do not make demands."

"I saw the inside of the gag when I freed you. I saw the inscription. The glyphs that made up the curse, including a distinctive capital H — like the one for the Hull Corporation."

She scrunched her brow and looked over at Tucker. He put his hands in his pockets. "You're going to start believing him? Please. You know better. What kind of curse would require me to put my initials in it?"

Dr. Connor squinted at Max. He scooted away from her and said, "No curse — probably. But I have no doubt that the gag itself was the property of the Hulls. Which makes it highly unlikely that anybody else had access to it that could make use of it."

In a swift motion, Dr. Connor crossed to the iron gag. Max caught sight of Drummond's stunned face. He wanted to signal the ghost, tell him to be ready to move, but his partner was too shocked by the loss of Leed and the bizarre situation to notice.

"Stop," Tucker said, and Dr. Connor halted less than a foot from the gag.

She hissed. "You don't want me to look in there? Something to hide?"

"I only want you to understand the consequences of such an action. I have taught you and your family many things about magic, made you more powerful than most, but I have not shared everything. You are in a delicate state right now. Surely, you can feel the energy heating inside of you. If you are not careful, you may hurt yourself more than you realize."

"I only want to know who is responsible for what happened to me."

"You know that answer already. Max Porter."

Like a rabid animal, she shot towards Max.

Max pointed at the gag. "Look for yourself! I'm not afraid of you checking it because it's not my magic that marks it."

She turned back toward the gag. Her skin glowing hotter each time. Max feared that whatever sanity she had left was boiling away.

Tucker snapped his fingers at her. "I forbid you to look in that gag."

This stopped her. She hovered above the cursed iron but her eyes no longer sought it. Her shoulders slumped as she said through gritted teeth, "You forbid me?"

"You are not ready to know what is written inside there."

Max thought he heard her sniffle as she said, "Even after my death, you still find ways to betray me."

"And you still find ways to fail me."

"My family served you —"

"You Connor women." With a disdainful sneer, he spit over his shoulder. "I only ever put up with the lot of you because you handle magic better than most. But I would've been better off training a dog. At least that kind of bitch knows how to be loyal."

Dr. Connor roared as she appeared to take some of the firelight away. The air around her darkened. She was a ghost pushed too far. She was losing control, falling into the madness that created evil spirits and poltergeists.

Max felt a tug at his arm. Sandra urged him to move back.

"Out of the circle," she whispered. "She's turning — like what almost happened to Drummond once. Remember?"

"Not the kind of thing I'm likely to forget."

A horrid squeal erupted from the depths of Dr. Connor, and flames burst from her ghostly skin. Leaving a smoking trail behind her, she barreled her way toward Tucker. He stood his ground. When she reached him, he grabbed hold of her burning hair and swung her down. She smashed right through him and back into the air, leaving him gasping on the charred ground.

The Pale Man, his hands shaking wildly, shot his gun at her. Dr. Connor swooped over to him and punched a burning fist into his chest. Like a witch at the stake, the Pale Man burst into flames. With his head ablaze, he dashed into the woods.

The smell of sulfur filled the air. Black and white smoke billowed off of Dr. Connor, creating a thick fog. Max and

Sandra covered their noses with their shirts while trying to keep low to the ground and out of sight.

Tucker's enraged grimace twisted as he spoke. "You think you can come after me?"

Dr. Connor took another run at him, but he plucked her out of the air and held her by the throat. Shock and rage fought upon her face. Her legs kicked out and her fingers dug into his arm, but her struggles only urged him to tighten his grip.

"I have studied magic for centuries. I am the most powerful, the most authoritative, and the most vicious practitioner you'll ever come across, and you think you have a chance against me? I live in two worlds — the living and the dead — and believe me, I know how to hurt people in both."

Fire spewed out of Dr. Connor like eruptions from the sun. They speared forward and burrowed into Tucker. He yelled but did not let go.

Sandra pointed Max's attention off to the side. Through breaks in the blowing smoke, Max saw that Mother Hope had entered the Tramping Ground. She had a large stick in her hand. With it, she drew a circle around herself, pushing the lines deep enough into the earth so that it would not be easily broken. Within the circle, she drew a triangle and knelt in the center.

He could see the determination in her eyes even as she fumbled the stick and had to push her face close to the ground to find it again. She stayed there, bent over the charred earth, as she inscribed the triangle with whatever spell she planned.

A thick volume of fire poured out of Dr. Connor and crossed the sky, dropping onto Mr. Pescatore. He never made a sound. One moment he lay where Drummond had dropped him, and the next moment, only a burning puddle remained.

Leon rushed out, hobbling on his injured leg. He tried to pull Mother Hope back, but she smacked him with her stick. "I have to do this. We'll all die if she's not stopped." Mother Hope sat back on her knees, closed her eyes, and mumbled words in a soft voice.

Drummond zipped behind her and settled next to Max.

"This is out of control. You guys better go. I'll let you know what happened."

Max liked the idea, but Sandra shook her head. "It's too late. If we run now, one of these people will take over everything. We'll have to keep running. Forever. Someone is going to get all the power tonight, and if we're ever going to have a life here or anywhere, then we've got to be involved with how this all plays out."

Dr. Connor's screech lit up the air as she arched back and fire volcanoed from her mouth. Her eyes burst as her body seized. Tucker howled like a warrior calling upon all his reserve strength. With his bare hands, he shredded Dr. Connor's ghost body apart as though tearing paper. A bright flash exploded from within her. Max shielded his eyes until the last of her haunting screams dissipated into the night along with all trace of her existence.

Darkness settled in amongst the smoldering wood. Watching Tucker stride toward Mother Hope, Drummond said, "I don't think this is playing out all that well for us."

Chapter 26

LIKE A HULKING BEAST, Tucker moved in. Max half-expected the Hull patriarch to pound his chest and roar. No need to intimidate, though. Mother Hope's chin vibrated faster than the words pouring out of her mouth. She clenched her hands against her stomach, kept her focus on the words she inscribed on the ground, and kept repeating them. Faster, faster.

Tucker planted his feet on the edge of her circle. "You have lost. Bow before me and pray for my mercy."

Sandra watched with her mouth agape. "We can't let him win this. We can't."

Drummond said, "Doll, I agree. What do you want to do?"

She shook her head, her eyes glued to the battle before her.

"Bow and I shall let you live." Tucker raised a fist, ready to strike.

Mother Hope, her mouth still rambling out words, gazed up at him. She shoved her fist into the air, and a pale light shimmered between her fingers. "Leave, Unclean Spirit! Return to the dead! You don't belong here. You never have. You never will."

Tucker covered his eyes and stumbled back. Max's heart leaped. He wanted to rush out there and cheer on Mother Hope, forgive her for all she had done to him, anything as long as she finished Tucker Hull forever.

But then Tucker stopped. He looked at his arm. He was not injured. Stomping back towards her, he finally let loose his roar.

Mother Hope flinched as Tucker grabbed her frock and threw her aside. She tumbled into Leon, knocking them both down. Stepping around her circle, Tucker thundered upon them.

Leon held Mother Hope against his chest. Blood dribbled from her head as her limbs shivered in his arms. Tears streamed down his cheeks.

Even from across the Tramping Ground, Max could see Leon's body returning to its rightful age. With glistening, wrinkled eyes, Leon looked up at Tucker. "Please. Let us go. Let me get her to a hospital. You've won. She's nothing against you now. Just an old lady."

Max reached into his pocket and pulled out the canister. His stomach twisted. Facing Sandra, he kissed her hard. "I don't know what's going to happen, but you're right — there's nobody left to do anything but us."

Her face paled. "No, Max. Don't do anything stupid."

"Come on. It's me." He winked at her, though he felt no mirth, and dashed for Mother Hope's circle.

As he ran, he unscrewed the top of the container. He threw the lid aside and felt liquid slosh out onto his hand. Just a few more feet. He had no clue what to do after that, but getting to the circle was the important first step.

Leon looked straight at Max and no amount of waving turned him away. Tucker whirled around and made an overhand motion as if throwing a ball. Though Max saw nothing, he felt it. Something hard like a lead weight slammed into his shin and his feet no longer were underneath him.

As he hit the ground, all he could think was *Don't drop the canister!* He succeeded in that much. But with the lid gone, the liquid shot out and along with it, the eyeball that once belonged to the witch, Marlyn Chester.

The eyeball floated through the air and settled on the edge of Mother Hope's circle. Max and Tucker locked their gazes. Both launched for the eye, but the invisible weight that had knocked Max down now wrapped around his ankle. He could barely move. Tucker, however, moved like a ravenous animal. Eyes wide and alert. Drool streaming from his mouth.

With a swift motion, he snatched the eyeball and stabbed it into the air like a champion holding a trophy. Laughing, he strolled around the circle. "I was going to take out Mother Hope's eyes, but thanks to Max Porter, I've got the power I need. And if ever I need more, Mother Hope will still be a useful donor. Thank you, Max, thank you."

He shot his arm into the sky again and smiled. He never saw Drummond. The ghost bowled into Tucker, leading with his right shoulder. Tucker gasped as the eye slipped from his grip. Before he struck the ground, Drummond crawled up and threw his own barrage of punches.

"You hit me hard before," the ghost said. "Allow me to return the favor."

Max pulled on his leg, trying to inch toward the eyeball; however, Sandra darted by him. She scooped up the eye and jumped into Mother Hope's circle.

"No," Max said. "You don't know what that'll do to you."

"You didn't know either. At least, I've had a little experience here." She knelt in the center of the triangle and before Max could protest more, she said, "Shut up. I've got to read what Mother Hope wrote in the dirt."

Drummond plunged his elbow into Tucker's chest. Tucker looked dazed, and Max felt the weight on his ankle release. He hopped to his feet and stormed toward Sandra.

"She's doing fine," Drummond yelled. Tucker had wrestled his way behind Drummond and locked his arms around the ghost's throat. "I could use a hand, though."

Max looked at Drummond and then Sandra. His wife pointed toward the center rocks. "Get the gag!"

Bounding to the center, Max grabbed the iron gag. Drummond flipped Tucker over and the two rolled in the dirt, throwing punches as they moved.

"Now what?" Max said, running back to Sandra.

Ignoring him, she muttered the words Mother Hope had written over and over. The eye sat cupped in her hands as she rocked back and forth. Max heard a painful crunch. He looked over to see Tucker standing while Drummond curled on the ground.

The head of the Hulls, the father of the entire line, the

magic-wielding patriarch bared his teeth at Max. "I had thought to let you live. But no more."

He charged like a bull. Max wanted to jump out of the way, but Sandra sat behind him. He heard her reciting the spell. The smell of burnt wood, usually a comforting aroma, turned his stomach. He lowered his body and charged forward.

The next seconds were a blur, and it was only weeks later that Max fully understood what had happened. He remembered running with his head down, cringing at the expectation of smashing into Tucker Hull and possibly dying. Then the air lit up blindingly bright. Tucker skidded to a halt and stared beyond Max. Max stumbled and looked back.

Sandra shone like a sun.

In the sudden confusion, Drummond snapped up and clamped Tucker's arms behind him. Drummond kicked out the man's legs and wrenched his arms higher against his back. Tucker yelled, but Drummond yelled louder.

Like a reverent follower, Max knelt before his wife. He held out the iron gag. With an icy glare, she set the eye into the gag and covered it with her hand. The bright light surrounding her dissolved into her hand and then into the eye. A moment passed, and the gag glowed red before returning to its rusty form.

Covered in sweat and panting, Sandra flopped over. Max wanted to tend to her, but he knew this had to be finished first. He walked back to Tucker Hull.

"Okay, look," Tucker said, struggling against Drummond. "I see what you're thinking, but you've misunderstood this whole situation. Once I had all that power, I was going to share it with you."

"Hold still," Max said. "I suspect this will hurt a lot if you fight me."

"You can't do this to me. I won't allow it."

"Drummond."

The ghost shoved Tucker's arm, and Tucker arched forward, screaming but unable to move. Max shoved the gag over Tucker's mouth and pulled the iron strap back over his head. It was a tight fit, scraping hair and skin off of Tucker's skull, but it did fit.

Drummond let go of the man, and Tucker scratched at his own face, trying to remove the gag. He reached around the back of his head, but no matter what angle he came from, he could not pull off the cursed object.

With a jolt, he stopped. His arm flapped out. His leg kicked back. He turned to Max, his eyes searching for an answer to whatever strange sensations caused his body to spasm.

He clutched his heart and slumped over.

Drummond stared at the body, waiting. "That's it? After Dr. Connor, I was expecting something bigger."

Max didn't care about fireworks. He rushed over to Sandra. "Honey? You okay?"

She peered up at him and made a small smile. "I will be. After a long, hot bath and a bottle of Jack Daniels."

Chapter 27

MAX SAT IN THE DIRT and stroked Sandra's wet hair. Soon they would have to get up and deal with the consequences of the world, but for the moment, he was content to gaze into the eyes of his wife. Let the world and its consequences hang for a few minutes.

But soon those minutes vanished. Cecily Hull cried out as she rushed toward Tucker's body. She had an ax in her hand, and all Max could think was *where did she get that?*

Before anybody could move, she swung the ax and decapitated Tucker. She dropped the ax and picked up Tucker's head. Exhausted, she walked toward the path leading to the cars.

"Where do you think you're going?" Max said.

She stopped, and in slow steps, she turned back. "I'm in charge of the Hull family now. And I'm going to make sure this is properly taken care of."

Max eased away from Sandra. "That's not going to happen."

"Careful, Mr. Porter. Your help in this matter is appreciated, but don't try to cross me. I now have the full power of the Hull family at my disposal."

"Yeah, about that. When you get home, I think you'll find your family power substantially reduced."

"What?"

Max dug a business card out of his pocket. "It's amazing the people you bump into at a party. This card is for Brian Dorsett. Interesting fellow. Works for the Reynolds family."

"That ruse again?"

"Last time I was lying. This time, not so much."

"What did you do?"

"I did nothing. However, while we all played in the dirt out here, one of my younger associates delivered a file folder to Mr. Dorsett detailing the Hull family's involvement with the death of one of their cherished own — Z. Smith Reynolds. Now, I'm not exactly sure how things operate in these situations, but I'm pretty confident the Reynolds family has been itching for decades to find anything they could use to destroy the Hulls. From what I can tell, this is it. The investigations, the arrests, the unofficial retributions — I'm sorry to tell you this, but you've just inherited a family under siege."

Without realizing it, Cecily dropped Tucker's head. Then she passed out.

Leon's voice cut in. "No, ma'am, you shouldn't be walking. Let me carry you to the car."

"Nonsense," Mother Hope said, shuffling over to Max. "I'm a little shaken, that's all."

Max stepped in their way. "Don't be going for that head. I won't let you take it, either."

"I wouldn't dream of taking your prize. Just make sure you put it someplace nobody'll ever get to it."

"I promise."

She wagged her finger. "You haven't learned a thing. You shouldn't be making promises to me. Look what happened to you from the last time."

Max touched the mark on his chest. "I suppose now you'll tell me to give you Tucker's head or you won't remove this curse."

"I told you already, you get to keep the head. I'll keep the curse right where it is."

From behind, Sandra said, "You can't."

"Oh, I most certainly can, and I will. The Hulls are finished, but there's plenty of disorder that needs fixing. What better way for the Magi Group to continue its mission than with its own expert research firm on retainer."

Drummond threw his hat on the ground. "You've got to be kidding me." The hat vanished and reappeared on his head.

Mother Hope pushed by Max and, with Leon's help, negotiated her way down the root steps. "I'll give you a few days to recoup from this. Especially for your wife. That was an impressive display, dear."

Max grabbed Tucker's head. "We're not working for you. After I take care of this, we're done with your whole messed-up world of magic."

"Then you'll die." Mother Hope didn't bother looking back. Neither did Leon. They left the Devil's Tramping Ground, and a few minutes later, their car rumbled away.

As the sound died in the distance, Max placed Tucker's head in the bowling bag. Sandra rose and joined him. Drummond checked over the debris, making sure they didn't miss anything important, before he came over.

"Don't worry about this. From what I've heard in the Other, this place really has some serious magic. All the bodies, the blood, everything will disappear by morning."

Max looked at his feet. "Maybe we shouldn't be standing in here, then."

"Look at you. Suddenly a crybaby." Drummond laughed and smacked Max on the shoulder. Both man and ghost let out a painful cry.

Rubbing his shoulder, Max said, "I guess the curse is back to being dormant."

"Come on," Sandra said, leading the way back to their car.

As they reached the gnarled roots, the ground rumbled.

"Everybody down!" Drummond yelled.

Max grabbed a tree and looked back. Tucker's headless body jittered as if suffering a seizure. His legs cracked, and Max thought the body might explode. Instead, the ground opened up beneath him. In seconds, it swallowed him whole, along with all the bodies and beer cans and debris, leaving behind nothing but solid earth.

Max might have stayed there for an hour staring at the strange land. But Sandra pulled him away. "Let's get out of here. I want my hot bath and booze."

Shaking off what he had seen, he said, "If we're going to be working for the Magi Group, I'm going to need a bottle for myself, too."

Drummond flew in front of them. "Hold on. I thought you said you wouldn't work for her."

"What can I do? I'm cursed." Max clasped Sandra's hand. "Besides, did you see what this great woman here did? She's got mojo like you wouldn't believe. With a witch like her for my wife, I think we can handle Mother Hope or anything else that comes our way."

With Sandra's head resting on his sore shoulder, they walked to their car. Max placed the bowling bag in the trunk. He planned to have Sandra find a good spell to cast on the bag that would prevent anybody from opening it with ease. Then he'd have the bag put into a safe deposit box. Then a spell on the safe deposit box. Maybe even a spell surrounding the bank vault.

As he drove for home, he thought of the old pilot's adage — *any landing you can walk away from is a good landing*. Well, they certainly walked away from this one. That would have to do for now.

A smile crept onto his lips.

Afterword

This was one of the more difficult Max Porter books to write for several reasons. There were logistical issues within the book that were challenging, such as the big finale in which I had to juggle ten characters, almost all of which had full stories that needed to be addressed in some way. The book also presented the challenge of wrapping up everything that came before while opening a door to a new future for Max, Sandra, and Drummond. Oh, and I still had to put in a bit of history and mystery. Hopefully, you've enjoyed the book enough to feel satisfied by my efforts.

As for truth versus fiction — here are a few answers: The big one first. The death of Z. Smith Reynolds and the resulting murder charges against his wife, Libby Holman, is true. Marlyn Chester is a figment of my imagination, but all the other names related to the case were real people. There are a handful of books that go into great detail about the case, and it's fascinating to see how wealth and fame altered the path of justice in this situation.

Libby Holman's story is also true. Though not cursed by a witch, she did live a life both blessed and cursed — a life she ended on her own terms. You can search her name on YouTube and hear the recordings of her big hits. Knowing how her life turned out can make her deep voiced singing rather eerie, but if that doesn't bother you, the music is worth listening to.

Also in the truth department is the Devil's Tramping Ground. You can find pictures online and read numerous tall tales about the area. Unless you're a diehard fan of this series or weird locales in general, I don't recommend seeking this place out. Not because of any fear over the place itself, but rather because it is not nearly as exciting to see as it is to read about. It's an empty circle of land in some woods just off of a backroad. It's also a pain to find. Even with a GPS.

As always, thank you for spending your time with me, Max, Sandra, and Drummond. We'll be back with more as soon as we recover from this latest adventure. Take care.

Acknowledgements

There are always numerous people involved in helping make a book happen. Special thanks goes to Jeff Dekal for another amazing cover, Ed Schubert for friendship and support, my Launch Team for their enthusiasm and error catching, especially Lisa Gall, Randy Wood, and Sarge, and of course, to Glory and Gabe.

Most of all, my enduring thanks to you, my reader. Max, Sandra, and Drummond have become far more than I ever expected because of you. For the first time, I'm daring to think well beyond the next few books for our trio. So, as long as you keep coming back, I've got some wonderful plans in store!

Thank you for making this possible.

About the Author

Stuart Jaffe is the madman behind *The Max Porter Paranormal Mysteries,* the *Nathan K* thrillers, *The Malja Chronicles, The Bluesman, Founders, Real Magic,* and so much more. He trained in martial arts for over a decade until a knee injury ended that practice. Now, he plays lead guitar in a local blues band, *The Bootleggers,* and enjoys life on a small farm in rural North Carolina. For those who continue to keep count, the animal list is as follows: one dog, three cats, three aquatic turtles, one albino corn snake, seven chickens, and a horse. As best as he's been able to manage, Stuart has made sure that the chickens and the horse do not live in the house.